Tales in Sombre Tones

Stories by Sean Walter

Illustrations by Karen Ruffles

of Drawing in Dark

Sean would like to dedicate this book to Courtney,
who always enjoyed and encouraged his work.

Karen would like to dedicate this book to Socks,
for the use of her bridle
And to Schroe the snake, for modeling.

Table of Contents

1. Scavengers — 1
2. Fairy Tales — 7
3. Addictions — 15
4. Jinxed — 23
5. The Deal of a Lifetime — 29
6. Lost at Sea — 37
7. The Warmth of Illusion — 45
8. Hunted — 57
9. Name Your Poison — 69
10. To Spite the Living — 77
11. Don't Look — 87
12. Finders Keepers — 95
13. A Question of Evil — 103
14. Mercurial — 111
15. Cages — 117
16. Charmed — 127
17. The Borrower — 135
18. In an Instant — 141
19. Timber — 151
20. To Catch a Kelpie — 161
21. Unconscious Mistakes — 169
22. Instinct — 175
23. The Creature's Lament — 185
24. Rust and Dust — 199

About the author

One would think, since this is my second book of short stories, that I would have gotten the hang of introducing myself. Well, I haven't. I have no excuse, so bear with me.

I was born and raised in Portland, Oregon – yes, that Portland, which is nearly nothing like it is portrayed on television or online. Portland has a dark history and a disturbing underbelly, which I have been comfortable in and around for most of my life.

I have worked here as a bartender, a bodyguard, a white-glove furniture deliveryman, security for orgies, a clerk, as protection for a call girl, a crate-maker, a janitor, a bouncer, and as an EMT. I've met many good people, far more bad ones, and so many who are indifferent that it boggles the mind.

I've started to travel, to meet new and interesting societies, and to make friends with them. I still study people whenever possible. I still keep their lies and their secrets. My hoard grows, even now. One might wonder what I'm going to do with it all...

About the Artist

Karen Ruffles lives in the coastal town of Whitby in the UK, a perfect location for an artist with a love for the gothic side of horror. Working as Drawing in Dark, she specialises in charcoal and carbon pencil drawings covering a wide range of subjects but her first love is the monsters who wander into her studio and in some cases, take up permanent residence. One of them brought a suitcase.

About the book

In this book, I wasn't alone with my nightmares. I had Karen's along as well. She has taken stories of mine and created haunting masterpieces with them, and I have taken monsters of hers and told their tales.

Herein, you'll find demons, dragons, old gods, ancient creatures, and nightmares that don't want to die. Be warned.

They say there is power in words, and I must agree, because some of the creatures in this book have come to visit me. Some of them, even now, are roaming free, wandering, looking for a new mind to inhabit.

Yours looks cozy.

Scavengers

Emily walked along the narrow forest road on her way home. The night had not been going well. Her date for the evening, a bullish man named Collin, had picked her up from her home and they had gone to a party in the next town over. The party had started pleasantly enough, but after a few drinks, Collin became more and more forward with his advances toward her.

When he groped at Emily after already being told off for it twice, she punched him square in the nose. She had broken it. She was certain because noses aren't supposed to look that way, and besides, she had felt the cartilage snap under her fist. Nobody at the party would give her a ride home, so she began to walk. That was a half hour ago. She kicked a stone down the pavement and it fell into the roadside ditch with a splash. She glared at it.

Light spilled around her from behind and a familiar car sped past. Emily ducked into the forest and behind a tree as the car screeched to a halt. Collin's drunken voice called from the road. "Emily!" There was anger there, soaked in alcohol.

Emily briefly entertained the idea of finding a very large rock to beat Collin senseless with, but thought better of it. *If I can avoid this idiot, all the better. But when I get home, I'm going to the police,* she promised herself. Her mind made up, she ran into the forest.

The moon was full and light made its way through the sparse canopy with ease, so she was able to keep up a quick pace. By her reckoning, her home was less than five miles in the general direction she was headed. She would be there in no time at all.

But the forest grew denser the further she went into it, the canopy grew thicker, and soon she lost the light. Collin was still shouting from somewhere behind her, following her by sheer luck. Still moving quickly, though blindly, through the undergrowth, she ran into a low branch that snapped from the trunk. She stumbled, righted herself, then grabbed the fallen branch for protection. Dark or not, she knew roughly how tall Collin was, and could easily locate his head with her new club.

Up ahead of her the forest thinned into a clearing, illuminated by the moonlight. Reasoning that seeing a pissed-off woman with a large stick might just scare even an absolute moron like Collin, she made for the clearing.

She was only a few yards into it before she fell.

The first sensation was the cold – like ice engulfing her whole body, pushing the air out of her lungs. She breathed in from the shock and took-in a lungful of putrid water. She dropped her club in her scrambling to gain purchase on something, anything to get to the air once again. Finally she was able to surface, coughing and gagging on the water. She kicked in her heavy boots and swam in the direction of the shore. She pulled herself onto the muddy, grassy earth and promptly threw up.

Emily saw nothing for several seconds as she lay on the shore, coughing out the water she had inhaled, and then she remembered Collin and jolted upright. There was some rustling in the under-brush across the small pool, and she knew Collin had heard her fall. She searched the shore for anything she could use as a weapon, but something in the water caught her eye.

Her mind immediately jumped to the thought that it was an alligator with how it insinuated itself along the surface of the water, but even in this low light she could tell that this was no alligator. It moved too quickly, and with too much determination. *Besides,* she thought, as logic kicked in, *alligators don't live in this part of the world.*

And then, none of that mattered anymore. The pain in her lungs disappeared, her anxiety vanished, and all was calm. Even the om-inous, dark pool with its unknown creature seemed comforting to her. It was as if every care in the world suddenly didn't matter – not Collin, not the thing in the water swimming closer, not even surviv-ing. She didn't even care how or why it had happened.

The creature breached the water, and it was beautiful. Its green hair, its elongated eyes, the almost humanlike torso it used to climb onto the shore, dragging its gorgeous tail from the pool. Emily was absolutely captivated. She reached out to the smiling creature...

And Collin burst through the underbrush and stumbled, drunk-enly, into the pool. The creature turned, startled, and Emily could think clearly once again.

The edges of her vision, so soft a moment ago, hardened as real-ity took hold. Collin was thrashing about in the pool, and *something* was far too close to Emily. What she had taken to be hair appeared to be algae-encrusted tendrils. Its eyes were sheets of glass, wide, and un-lidded, taking in all light they could. The torso, while nearly human, was plated in scales, terminating in webbed hands. It smiled, constantly, unable to close its mouth from the size of its sharp teeth.

Emily raised her booted foot and kicked at the creature's head, sending it rolling into the water with a hiss. She stood up and retreated to the now inviting forest. From the safety of a tree, she turned.

Collin had stopped thrashing. He was holding-on to the eroded edge of the shoreline with one limp hand, and the creature was slowly rising from the water. Its shark-like tail flapped happily as it curled around Collin's torso. Collin pulled it toward him, pawing at what might have been breasts, then he leaned in and tried to kiss the creature.

It reacted in a flash. Its massive mouth opened, and it wrapped its long, sharp teeth around Collin's jaw. It pulled away, and the lower half of Collin's face went with it. But he didn't stir, he didn't scream or defend himself, he simply drew the creature closer, as if he were cuddling a loved one. A moment longer, and the blood-soaked monster sank its teeth into Collin's neck. Collin let go of the shore, and they both slipped beneath the water.

Emily wasted no time. She turned away from the pool and ran, bumping into trunks and bushes, running headlong into low branches, yet she kept going. When she emerged from the forest, she ran on. When she finally reached home, she locked the door behind her, gathered her breath for a moment, and screamed.

The coming days and weeks came with a search for Collin by the local police. They tried to question Emily about the fight at the party, but she only stared at the floor the entire time. The police documented her bruises and scrapes, thinking they understood, and left her in peace.

They searched the forest where his car had been located, but when two of the searchers vanished into it, they soon called it off.

For years to come, whenever someone went too far, whenever they were deemed to be beyond salvation, Emily would take them for a walk in the dense underbrush, and they would never be a problem to anyone ever again.

Fairy Tales

Since time immemorial, Whenever people have gathered together for warmth and drink, there would also be someone among them to tell tall tales. It's such a staple, such a commonplace occurrence the world over, that it is not difficult to imagine that the first pub came with a slightly loud, slightly grizzled old man who said that he had invented the pub years ago.

Ours was named Steve.

He could have been forty or four-hundred, never seemed to shave nor grow excess whiskers, and knew exactly fifteen jokes which he repeated time and again to anyone who would listen long enough. Those who knew him never warned the new victims of his particular style of humor. It was far more fun to let them suffer, to have them look at you with a face of confusion or of horror and silently mouth the words *Was that the joke?* in astonishment as the old man roared with laughter.

Tonight, Steve was in fine form. "I met the queen, once," he was saying to someone who hadn't asked as I walked in.

"What? Of England?" the woman asked.

"No, of course not," he started.

"But didn't you just-"

"I met the queen of the elves," Steve finished. The woman frowned at him in annoyance.

"...Right," she said, then turned back to her companion, whispered a quick conversation, and they both hurried away to a back table.

"Scaring people again, Steve?" I asked, taking the stool next to him.

"Some people just don't know a good thing when it comes along," he replied, smiling into his thin beer.

I made a face. "How can you drink that shit?" I asked. "It tastes like someone telling a story about a bad beer they had once being heard through a wall."

"It's thin, sure, but I can drink it all day." He laughed and, right on cue, started joke number eleven. "My dad always said this kind of beer was like making love in a canoe..." He paused, his smirk frozen in place as the bartender groaned. "It's fucking close to water!" he shouted, then slapped his own knee and started laughing again.

The bartender and I shared a look, and she sighed. "Porter?" she asked. I nodded.

"Oh, come on!" Steve yelled. "That was funny!"

I shook my head. "I was only a little funny the first time I heard it, but I was also a lot younger, then, and easily amused." I smiled at him as his face fell.

"Have I told you that before?" he asked.

"Twice this week," I replied, and laughed.

Steve paused. "Well, when you get to be my age, we'll just see how good your memory is."

"How old is that, anyway?"

"As old as my nose, and just a little bit older than my teeth." He laughed as I rolled my eyes.

Some time passed, and the beer flowed. Steve told six more jokes from his repertoire to unsuspecting customers as they ordered. Some laughed, politely. Others said nothing and wandered away in a hurry. Eventually, in desperation, I asked "Steve, don't you have any new stories?"

He leaned back in his chair and thought for a moment. "No," he replied, and laughed.

"Alright," I pressed on, "how about some old stories, then?"

He paused, his beer halfway to his lips, then he set it back down without drinking. "Old stories? I didn't think anyone wanted to hear old stories."

I shrugged. "Old or new doesn't much matter. So long as we haven't heard them before, we'll be happy."

"Really?" Steve asked. I nodded. "In that case, maybe I do have an old story for you."

I ordered another porter and some thin swill for Steve, then sat back to listen.

"Years ago," he began, "before all of this was here, before the houses got built, and the shopping districts, and before all these people came, this whole area was woodlands. The trees themselves weren't old – you didn't get old-growth trees around here, even back then – but the forest itself, as a whole, was ancient in the extreme.

"I had grown up on the outskirts of the forest, spending my

days helping out with the chores when I wasn't in school. But, you should know, back in those days, school was a thing you attended when you could, when your chores and life allowed it. The wealthy families all had private tutors for their children, while the rest of us made do with whoever was capable of reading and who could write and do math for that week."

I looked at the bartender, confused, and she only shrugged. "How long ago was this?" I asked.

"Don't interrupt," Steve replied, then continued. "The only school in the area was through a thinning in the forest, along an old dirt trail that was used, mostly, by those who wanted to get to and from our collection of homes and farms. We weren't really a village in those days. We didn't have any official name or local government. If pressed, we would say that we belonged to the next town over. So, it wasn't strange that my school was so far from home, and it wasn't odd that I should be gone from sunrise to well after sunset. It was simply how things were done.

"One day, just as the sun was rising, I set off for town for a day of schooling. I remember how thick and cold the morning dew was that day. My coat was heavy with it by the time I reached the forest.

"It was dark there, in the trees, and my path was lit only sporadically by the rays of dawn, but I was cold and on a mission, and took very little notice. The path went through the narrowest part of the forest, but it wound and meandered around the growths of trees wherever carts could find a route, so the journey itself was several miles long. I knew the path by heart, could even follow it in the dark, so I wasn't worried.

"That is, of course, until the singing started."

Steve took a long pull from his thin beer, then continued.

"It was a kind of rhyme, to my ear, but I couldn't make it out.

The song came from a ways off the path, where the trees and under-brush grew thick, but my curiosity drove me to find it. My coat, an over-sized ordeal I had inherited from my father when he no longer had a use for it, caught and snagged on a bramble bush. The singing was nearby. Some of the words were beginning to make sense, and I felt an odd urge to press-on, with or without my coat. So, I left it hanging there in the brambles. I remember thinking the air wasn't nearly as cold the further I moved away from the path.

"A few minutes of stumbling in the dark further, and I found myself in a glade. Light shown through the branches above, but the forest here was strange. Branches and trunks grew at odd angles. One was almost horizontal, and attached to it was a simple plank and rope swing.

"It was quiet, but it was a pregnant silence. The kind of silence that only comes with somcone or something trying incredibly hard not to be heard. The singing had stopped, but it was almost as if the vibrations of their voice could still be felt in the air.

"The wind blew through the glade, and the swing began to gently sway. A whisper came from the darkness, but I couldn't make it out. A deeper, steadier whisper replied to the first. 'Hello?' I called out, hoping I hadn't scared them. 'I just wanted to see who was singing. I didn't mean to startle you.' I moved further into the clearing, out into the light, so whoever was there could see me.

'Did you like it?' a voice asked from behind me. I turned and staggered and caught my hand on a sharp branch, cutting my palm as I fell. I stood up and pressed my wounded hand to my shirt, instinctively. When I regained my composure, I looked back to see a young girl, no older than I was, coming into the light. She was barefoot, I remember thinking how odd that was, and her thin features and dark skin caught my eye.

"'Was that you? The singing, I mean?' I stammered.

"She nodded enthusiastically. 'Did you like it? I've been practicing for a long time.' Her voice was soft and bright. It reminded me of springtime.

"'It was beautiful,' I said. She smiled at me, and I was lost. All thought of continuing onward to school was forgotten. She walked past me to the swing, but strangely, never once settled down to her heels, her toes gripping deep into the mossy earth. 'What was it you were singing? I couldn't understand it.'

"She sat down at the swing and began to gently sway in the breeze. 'It's from an old song that's from an old place. I'm not sure it translates to your language very well.'

"I went and sat down on a stone nearby the swing, watching her sway back and forth, admiring the grace of her movements. She began to hum the same tune I had heard as I approached, and I felt as if I was wrapped in warmth. I must have been hypnotized by the movement, or the humming, or her beauty, because I was soon fast asleep."

Steve paused as his next beer arrived, seemingly lost in thought or in memory, back in that glade once again. After another long pull on his beer and a sigh, he continued.

"I dreamed, then. I dreamed of strange creatures made out of earth, and others out of plants, and of elves, and fairies, and demons of fire and ice, and people made of pure light, and others made out of the night sky... I couldn't make sense of it all as it marched by me, but I heard her singing, on and on, through it all.

"I awoke in total darkness. My head rested in her lap, and she gently stroked my hair as she sang. I tried to lift my head, to get up, but it was as if a force were holding me down.

"'Shhhh...' she whispered. 'You're safe here.'

"I tried to respond, but nothing came out, and I was so very tired. I barely felt the needle-like claws gently raking at my skin, nor the tingle of my senses slowly fading away. Somewhere in the darkness, a deep voice growled and rumbled, and then I passed out once again.

"I awoke to the sound of an axe on wood, in stark daylight so bright that it was blinding. I felt stiff, as if I hadn't moved from an uncomfortable position in days. I was still in the glade, but it was different, somehow. Memories of fantastic creatures and nightmares turned flesh kept flashing before my eyes. I stood, disoriented, confused, and looked around. Everything seemed smaller, somehow. I was dressed in strange fabrics and silks, and my hand had healed.

"Somewhere behind me, off in the distance, beyond the now rotted ropes of the swing, I could hear her, giggling at my confusion.

"It took me some time to realize it, but years had passed as I slept, if I was ever asleep at all. I have the feeling that whatever she was, she stole most of my memories from those years."

Steve looked around at the bartender and me, as if surprised to see we were still listening, and he smiled. "That's all, I'm afraid."

The bartender shook her head and turned away to wipe the far side of the bar. I looked at Steve for several seconds, studying his face. "How much of that story was true, Steve?" I asked.

He turned to me, his usual grin on his face, and said "How much do you believe?" Then he set some money on the bar for his drinks, nodded to me, and turned to leave, humming a strange tune to his own delight.

Addictions

The night was cool. Wind came from the east, blowing ash and sparks down the dark, deserted street.

It had to be done. He knew that. There was simply no alternative. If he hadn't done it, someone else, surely, would have come along to do it in his stead. But it had to be him. He didn't have a choice.

The lights and sirens flew past him as he walked into a mounting fog. *Just this last one,* he thought. *I can quit after this.* He meandered, taking a left here, a right there, twisting and turning his way along, going further from that inferno he started and the horrors within. It wasn't until he stubbed his toe and tripped on a hidden curb that he realized just how thick the fog had become. He pulled himself up and sighed, and the sound of his own breath seemed dull and far, far away – like a cat hissing through velvet pillows.

He had never liked cats, he mused as he began to walk once more. They always seemed to know more than they should, as if they were witness to his past, as if they could comprehend what he had done and had chosen to condemn him for his deeds. That woman had a cat. It was what had captured his attention in the first place, days ago, as he passed in the night.

The cat had been left out, and he spotted it scratching and complaining at the front door to the house. It had quieted when he approached, and looked up at him with pleading in its eyes.

He had simply let it in.

And that had been that.

Another turn, and he narrowly avoided walking into a signpost. He held his hand at arm's length and marveled at the fact that he could no longer see it. Street lights formed small, bright cones above his head, but the light barely reached him. He wondered, briefly, if he had walked out of the world, and if he would ever be found again by any living creature – the muted world of the fog folding around him, holding him, hiding him from the world of the living.

He laughed at the absurdity of it all and heard a woman gasp just in front of him, hidden by the mist. He smiled at his fortune.

"Oh, I'm sorry miss," he said, in what he thought of as his most charming voice. "I was enjoying not being able to see my own feet in this weather. Did I frighten you?"

The woman in the fog laughed nervously. "No, I'm alright. I just didn't see you there. I nearly ran into you!"

"What a tragedy that I laughed when I did, then," he smiled, then remembered that he needn't bother.

"...Right," came the reply after a moment. "Look, do you happen to have a lighter? My matches are useless in this damp."

He dug in his pocket for his lighter and held it out to where he had heard her voice, then flicked it to life. He stared at the flame, reduced in clarity but just as beautiful as the blaze it had started. He could almost hear the screams of the woman within the flame, and see how she had stirred and flailed against her bonds, as she burned, in the dancing of it.

Out of the fog, on the very edge of vision, a cigarette emerged. It struck the flame and roused him from his reverie. He laughed again. "You know, there's something a little unsettling about a disembodied cigarette seeking a light from out of the fog," he said.

"Is it better than what looks like a severed hand offering you a lighter?" she replied.

"Fair point." He hesitated for what he hoped what just long enough, then added "I hate to ask, but I don't suppose you know where we are right now?"

The woman laughed. "I was hoping you knew. I've been wandering in this mess for what seems like ages. Are we near to high street, do you think?"

He turned his head to look back on where he had come, and couldn't tell one direction from another save for the glow of the streetlights above. "Your guess is probably better than mine. I'm not from around here." He tried to sound as pathetic as possible.

"Oh, you poor thing," she started, and he smiled to himself. "How did you end up here?"

"I quite enjoy walking in the fog. When I saw this rolling-in, I just couldn't resist," he lied. "What about you?"

"I just wanted to take a walk to cool off. It was too hot inside."

He smiled once again at a private joke. Aloud, he said "Would you like to stumble along blindly together?"

"I don't know. You might be an axe murderer," she joked.

"Only on Saturdays. This being Wednesday, you're perfectly safe."

She laughed. "It's Thursday."

"Even better! Those are for drownings."

She laughed once more. "Alright, fine. But you better not lead me into any walls."

"You have my word," he said. "No walls."

They began walking, unsteadily, in the damp, grey air. Every few steps she made her presence known by taking a drag on her cigarette, making her appear in subtle orange shapes – here, a nose. There, a chin.

"So, where are you staying while you're in town?" the shapes asked.

"At the moment? Nowhere. I was staying with someone until a few hours ago, but that didn't work out, and I decided to leave."

"I know how that is. There's a small hotel somewhere around here, if we can manage to find it. You could probably stay the night there."

"Oh, I'll manage, I'm sure..."

They turned a corner, each following the other by sound alone. They talked on random subjects, the kind one talks to a complete stranger about to pass the time. Four times, as they wandered, they reverted back to the topic of the weather – how odd it was, how sur-real – and yet neither seemed to tire of it.

A car passed by, slowly, like a ship sailing an ocean of fog, only making itself known by its headlights. He caught the faintest image of her face in the glow. It was oddly familiar, like a half-remem-bered dream from years ago, the blanks filled in after each retelling with logical, purposeful ideas.

"Any closer and that thing could have killed us," he murmured.

"I'm sure we would have bounced off... probably."

Her face lit up with an orange glow once more as the embers came to life. Smoke flowed from her lungs a moment later.

"That's a really bad habit to have," he commented.

"Is it? I really just started earlier tonight."

"I wouldn't let it take hold, if I were you. I've always found habits near impossible to break, once I have them."

"And what habits have you got, then?" she asked.

He smiled. "I'll tell you about it later. In the meantime, could you blow that away from me? I can't stand the smell of smoke."

She laughed, loudly.

"What's so funny?" he asked.

"You are. How can you say that you don't like the smell of smoke?"

"I just never have. I don't see how that's funny."

"You're obsessed with fire and hate smoke. I think that's hilarious." She laughed again.

"I always burn things on my way out, that way I don't have to smell it much," he said.

"I see. That way, you can enjoy the flames from a distance, is that it?"

"...Exactly."

They walked on for a few moments.

"How did you know I enjoyed fire?" he asked, finally.

"You'd be amazed what you can learn after spending a few days with someone." Her voice was harsh, almost ashen in the sound.

"Days? It's been an hour at most, I'm sure." He chuckled.

Her face glowed orange in the fog once more, brighter than before.

"You're not lighting up another one, are you?" he asked.

But the glow didn't fade. It held there, then seemed to spread to the fog around them. He watched as her skin cracked and peeled, blooming in firelight from within. She exhaled a plume of thick, black smoke. The air became oppressively hot, and he fell to his knees, coughing into his sleeve. He tried to crawl away, but she reached out her hands and grabbed him by the wrists, holding him in place like a vice, torching his flesh wherever she touched him.

The flames spread all around them. His lungs burned, his vision blurred and faded, and the roar of the fire filled his ears. He screamed until he could no longer breathe, struggling to inhale through seared-off lips and burned lungs. Just before he fell unconscious, she pulled him into an embrace, scorching every inch she touched, and whispered in his ear *"Just this last one. I can quit after this..."*

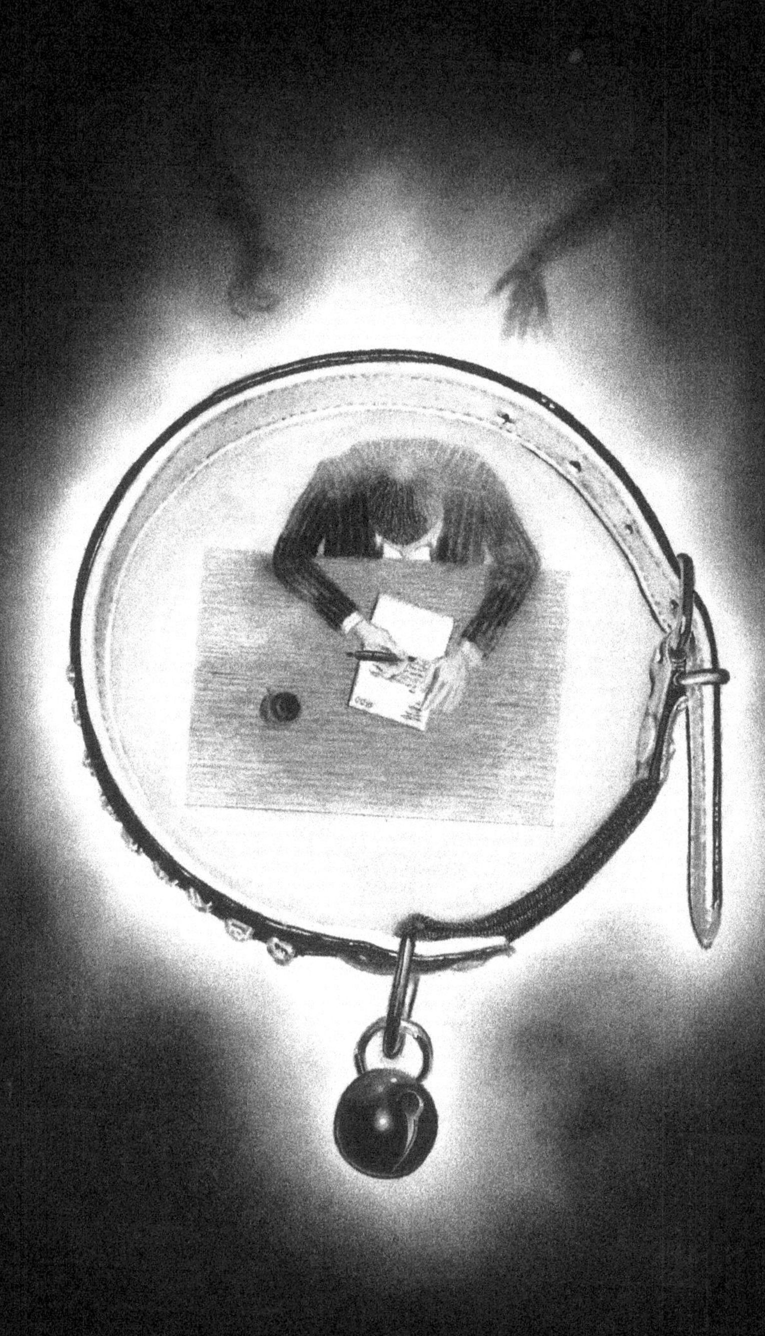

<u>Jinxed</u>

If the moon hadn't been full, Oscar was sure, none of this would be happening. He wouldn't have dreamed of harpies stalking him from the rooftops, he wouldn't have slept through his alarm and been late to leave for work, and he wouldn't have spilled his coffee down his shirt as he wove in and out of traffic.

But it was a full moon.

Oscar decided that his bad luck was being compounded by the moon. It was as if the last thirty-one years of life having been lived so carefully, avoiding spilling salt, hanging horseshoes (points up) around his house, and never once having broken a mirror had annoyed the powers that be, and they had simply been waiting for an opportunity to attack him while he was vulnerable.

He turned onto his office building's street, but his eye was drawn to an alleyway he'd never noticed before. It appeared no different than any other, and yet he felt compelled to stop his car and explore it. He saw a black cat from the corner of his eye run from the sidewalk and in front of his car. He swerved at the very last moment, avoiding the cat and cursing his further bad luck.

He parked, collected his backpack full of work materials, and stepped out of his car. And there he saw the same black cat waiting patiently across the street, sitting on the stairs to his office building. It was staring right at him, tail twitching this way and that, waiting to ambush him once again. Oscar cautiously approached the entrance, trying to avoid the cat's eyes. He nearly jumped out of his skin when the cat let out a small "Prrrb?" and put one paw forward, hesitated, then sat back down once again.

Shaken, Oscar took a deep breath, closed his eyes, and dashed through the door. He slammed it closed behind him, then rested against it while he caught his breath.

"Reow!" came the call from the other side of the door, along with several seconds of scratching against the doorframe. Oscar bolted up the stairs to his office.

The morning carried on as it had begun. Oscar messaged the wrong client and exposed the preferential price of another, resulting in a contract loss for the company. He then opened a chain letter in his email that was alarmingly close to being past the deadline for sending on, and before he could finish forwarding it, he computer froze. By the time it was rebooted, the deadline had passed. He dropped his head in his hands and sobbed.

Already behind and having infuriated his boss by his earlier mistakes, Oscar decided to eat lunch at his desk. He worked studiously while mechanically chewing his bologna on rye. He finished and went to throw away the sandwich wrapper in a trash bin below a window which looked out into the street three floors below. He glanced out of the window and saw his car, safely tucked where he had left it. And there on the hood, curled up in a mockery of innocence, lay the void of the black cat with the expression of pure contentment.

Oscar stared down at it for several moments, scowling, wondering what he had done to deserve today and if he could avoid it in the future.

The afternoon passed slowly, Oscar's work crawling along at a jagged pace, burdened by his constant worry. In his mind, unbeknownst to him, the cat had somehow found a way inside his car and now waited in the back seat, ready to pounce on him as he drove home and cause a fatal accident. He wondered if *Death by Cat* was a common problem.

Night fell. The workday was coming to a close, and Oscar was worried. He packed his bag slowly, carefully, not sure what else this day would bring him. He went down the stairs and inspected the scene through the building's glass exit doors. The black cat was still there, its eyes glowing in the low light as it rolled around playfully on top of his car.

Oscar waited until the cat was distracted by other passersby before he opened the door and began down the sidewalk, away from his car. It was several miles back to his home, but he could walk that. Perhaps he could get lucky enough to catch a bus, and then, in the morning, he could take a cab back to work. *Yeah,* he thought, *that will work.*

Something brushed against his leg. He looked down to see the black cat, purring loud enough to be heard over the passing cars, repeatedly rubbing itself against his slacks. Oscar jumped back and slammed into a wall, gasping in alarm. The cat sat down and cocked its head at Oscar, watching his desperate flailing and shooing motions with interest and amusement, but showed no signs of fleeing.

Panicked, Oscar edged along the wall, keeping the cat in view, watching for sudden movements. The mouth of an alleyway was just a few feet away. Oscar hoped to reach it before the furry evil that watched him with such intense curiosity could follow.

When he was within inches of the alley, the cat ran forward and began meowing for Oscar's attention. There was a pleading in its tone. When it saw that it was being ignored, it ran beyond the entrance to the alley and flopped over on its side, then rolled to its back, cocking its head to watch Oscar's reaction. Oscar turned into the alleyway and ran, leaving the cat and its insistent mews behind him. He smiled to himself. Finally, something was going right with his day.

The alley was dark and cold, the sunlight rarely reaching into its depths. Oscar walked along its unfamiliar twists and turns, pleased to have lost the black cat, but worried that he may have gotten himself lost at the same time. As he walked on, the place grew stranger.

He turned another corner, certain that this direction must lead to a main road, but where he expected to see people and cars, he only saw more narrow passageways between brick buildings. All of the trappings of humanity were around him – dumpsters in their usual place, odd bits of wind-blown trash stuck in piles here and there – but it somehow felt off. Sounds seemed to travel slower than they should. It was as if he was wandering through a physical echo of a location – something similar to the original, but subtly changed.

The alley grew darker as he went, a kind of subtle, insidious darkness that grew by degrees when not being watched. It took several more minutes before he noticed that there was nothing leading into this alleyway. No disused coal chutes, no one-way emergency doors, no windows or holes in the walls. He didn't know where he had been, nor how to return. The only way to proceed was forward into the maze of interwoven brickwork.

Oscar paused. Something had been drawing his attention for quite some time – something on the edge of hearing that suddenly made itself noticed. A sort of staggered whisper, soft words spoken quickly and rhythmically, filled the air. Out of the darkness ahead, Oscar watched a man in tattered clothes shamble toward him. The man was gibbering to himself, staring down into his hands as he shuffled along. Oscar tried to back away, only to find that his feet would not obey him. They stayed planted against the concrete no matter how much he pulled on them.

The stranger drew closer.

When he was a foot away, the man stopped. His hands slowly lowered from in front of his face and he raised his head. Oscar gasped. The man's eyes were nothing but black pits, absorbing every bit of light they could in this dismal place. It showed brown, jagged teeth through cracked lips in what Oscar could only assume was a smile, and then began to whisper, excitedly. "O-o-o-scar... O-o-o-o-scar," it called in a sweet voice. It reached out and caressed Oscar's face, repeating his name like a mantra. Finally, it gripped Oscar's chin in its fist. "Oscar... We've been waiting for you."

Its smile widened, its teeth grew, and its mouth opened...

The cat sat in the entrance to the alleyway, hopeful that the man would return, sad that she couldn't stop him from going in, and unsure why he had acted so strangely toward her. She waited until she heard the scream, and then she moved on. There was always a scream, but she waited, every time, just the same.

Maybe, she thought, she could save the next one that caught the alley's attention.

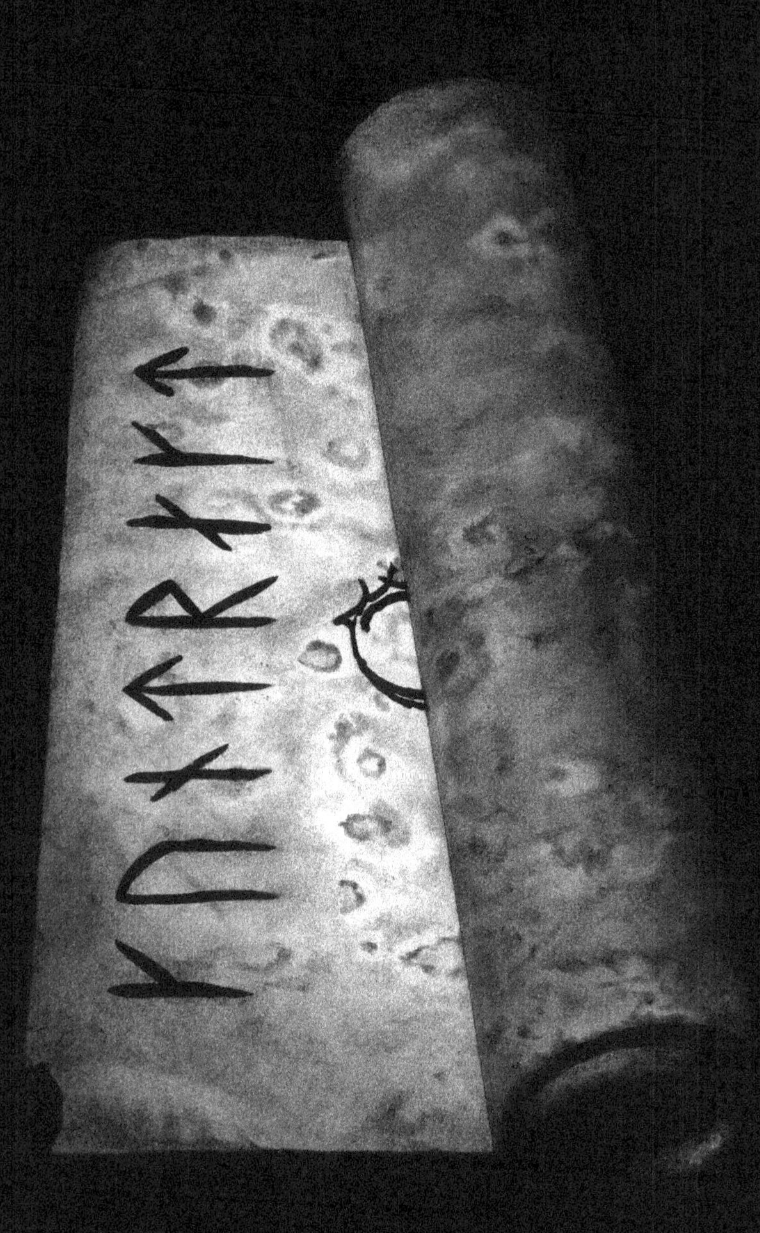

The Deal of a Lifetime

"It doesn't work that way anymore," the man had said. Joshua hadn't believed him, not about any of it, not then. But now...

It had been a bad day. Joshua's phone had given up the ghost sometime in the night, causing him to sleep through his alarm. He rushed into work as fast as he dared, breaking several traffic laws in the process. He arrived to his boss, Mr. Stoner, fuming behind the counter of the little clothing shop.

"Where the hell have you been?!" Mr. Stoner shouted, his multiple chins fighting for dominance on his face.

"Sorry, my phone died last night and I use that for my alarm." Joshua held up the black screened phone as proof." It won't happen again."

"You're god-damned right it won't! What if there had been a customer here, waiting for you to show up? What then?! Then we miss out on profits! No profit means no pay!"

Joshua wiped the bit of saliva off his face, and stared at Mr. Stoner, clenching his fist, considering his reaction. From behind him, a small, sweet voice asked "Excuse me? How much is this?"

Joshua nearly fainted with embarrassment. Before he could turn around to answer, Mr. Stoner pushed passed him and went toward the customer. "I'm terribly sorry," he said, his voice all milk and honey. "You know how it is with the youth these days. You can't make them *earn* an honest living even if you beat them with a stick!" He turned to glare at Joshua.

Joshua was seething for what remained of his shift.

After work, he headed for his girlfriend's house, hoping to get some sympathy for the day he'd had. On the way, he stopped at a repair shop. The sign out front, hanging on a rusty steel bar, blowing in the wind, read "We repair it all! Phones, computers, lives!" with a faded pyramid in the background. Joshua shook his head, and went inside.

The interior consisted of a small alcove, three chairs, a small sliding glass window with a bell sitting on the track, and a doorway leading further-in with a sign saying "Employees only." Nobody was there, so Joshua rang the bell.

"I can help you," a man who was standing alarmingly close to him said. "What model phone do you have?" he asked without being prompted as he went through the door and appeared behind the window.

The man didn't have the appearance of a repair technician. He wore a pinstriped suit, smartly fitted to his trim figure, complete with waistcoat, tie, and pocket square. His hair was greased upright and back, and stood in nearly identical rows upon his head.

Joshua handed him the broken phone. "It just died in the night," he said.

The man took it and began holding down one button while tapping at the screen with a stylus in a complicated pattern. When that failed to produce a result, he took the back cover off and examined the battery. Finally, he set it on the counter in front of him. "You have a real problem, sir," he said.

"What? Don't tell me you can't fix it."

"Oh, no. Your phone isn't broken. It's just depressed."

Joshua looked at the man. The man smiled back. He didn't appear to be a mad person. "My phone is depressed?" he asked.

"I'm afraid so. Worst case I've ever seen, too. But you're in luck! I know just how to fix it."

Joshua braced for the ridiculous repair fee that the man was sure to quote. "How?" he asked, holding his breath.

"It's really very simple. All you have to do, is kill your boss."

Joshua furrowed his brow. "What?"

"I'm afraid it's the only cure, at this stage. Before, it would have sufficed to simply find other employment, but after hearing how he treated you?" The man shook his head and shrugged. "Of course, what with you being a new customer, we could take care of that whole messy affair for you. Free of charge, as well. We believe very strongly in repeat business."

Joshua stared at what he now was certain was an escaped mental patient. Even though the thought of killing Mr. Stoner had come across his mind, he had never really considered it. "Um...okay," he stammered, confused and worried about upsetting the smiling madman behind the glass.

"Excellent!" the man said, joyfully. "We'll take care of everything. Don't you worry, sir!"

"...right," Joshua said, taking his phone back. "Well, I've got to go, now. Thanks for your help."

The man beamed. "Not at all! And do come back. I'm certain that we can help you again."

Joshua left the strange man and continued to his girlfriend's house. Once there, he got so wrapped up in telling her about Mr. Stoner that he forgot to mention the strange man wearing the suit in the repair shop. Beth, his girlfriend and woman of infinite compassion, listened to him and consoled him. Somehow, she always made him feel better.

Later that night, as Beth and Joshua slept in each others' arms, Joshua's phone rang. Still half-asleep, he answered it.

"What did I tell you, sir!" came the voice from the other end. "Now your phone is happy once again, and working just fine."

The day's events came rolling back to Joshua all at once. "What?" he breathed. "What did you do?"

"Why, only what we agreed to, sir. Your free introductory offer! We do apologize for the delay in service, but these things are best taken care of at night," the voice continued.

Joshua sat silent for several seconds. Eventually, he said "So, you're telling me that my boss is-"

"Eliminated! Yes, sir. We do hope you've enjoyed working with us, and do come in any time, should you have another problem that needs repairing. Goodnight, sir."

The line went dead. Joshua sat in bed, staring at his now perfectly functional phone. He used it to get online, and went to a local news website. Their current stories scrolled along in a sea of continuous information. "Breaking news: body found in local shop."

He read the details of the story with interest, and then, calmly, he turned off his pre-set alarm for the next morning.

Joshua awoke still confused about the events of the previous day. He thought about his boss, and was surprised at just how little he cared now that he was dead. He got up, got ready, and went back to the repair shop.

The not-so-mad man in the suit was waiting for him. "Hello again, sir! I see that you were most pleased with our first encounter. How can I help you today?"

Joshua glanced around the small, empty room. "What is this place?" he asked.

"Just a repair shop, sir. And, just like it says outside: *we repair it all!* Which reminds me, we do realize that last night's unfortunate events have left you wanting for work," the man said, still cheerful.

"I can always find more work," Joshua started.

"Of course you can, sir! No one is saying you can't. However, since we had some small part in your current circumstances, we wanted to offer you another deal."

"What kind of deal?" Joshua asked, curiosity getting the better of him.

"For starters, we will get you gainful employment – something that you'll not only enjoy, but will excel at! Secondly, we will pay you a small sum of monies as compensation for your lost wages and any unpleasant feelings you may be experiencing on the matter. Ten-thousand dollars, say."

Joshua laughed. "What do I have to do? Sign over my soul or something?"

The man in the suit smiled even wider than before. "It doesn't work that way, anymore," he said, and he explained how it *did* work.

Joshua started his new job a week later. The job itself was, as advertised, enjoyable in a way Joshua hadn't thought possible, and even he had to admit – he was very good at it. His work took him all over the world, and though he missed Beth from time to time, he was making enough money that by the end of the first year, they had bought a house together.

Soon, they started a family. Beth was able to quit her job and work on her own interests at home. They hired a nanny to take care of their kids.

Five years after starting his new life, Joshua received a promotion. No more would he have to travel all over the world for his work, which suited him just fine. He had been wanting more and more to be at home with Beth and the kids at night.

...now, he waited in his office, reminiscing about the last five years: all of the people he had changed, all of the circumstances he had improved, all of the lives he had ended, and he was proud to be so very good at his work. The man was right. It didn't work that way. None of it did.

"You see," the man in the suit had said, years ago. *"One soul is not enough. What is one soul, when you could have hundreds?"*

A pale, scared man opened the door to Joshua's office. It was his second visit, and he looked at Joshua without speaking.

"Thousands?"

The man took off his hat and wrung it in his hands, unsure of what to say. "Why did it have to be my wife? He choked on the word, and a tear streamed down his face.

"Millions."

Joshua smiled. "That's just what we agreed to, sir."

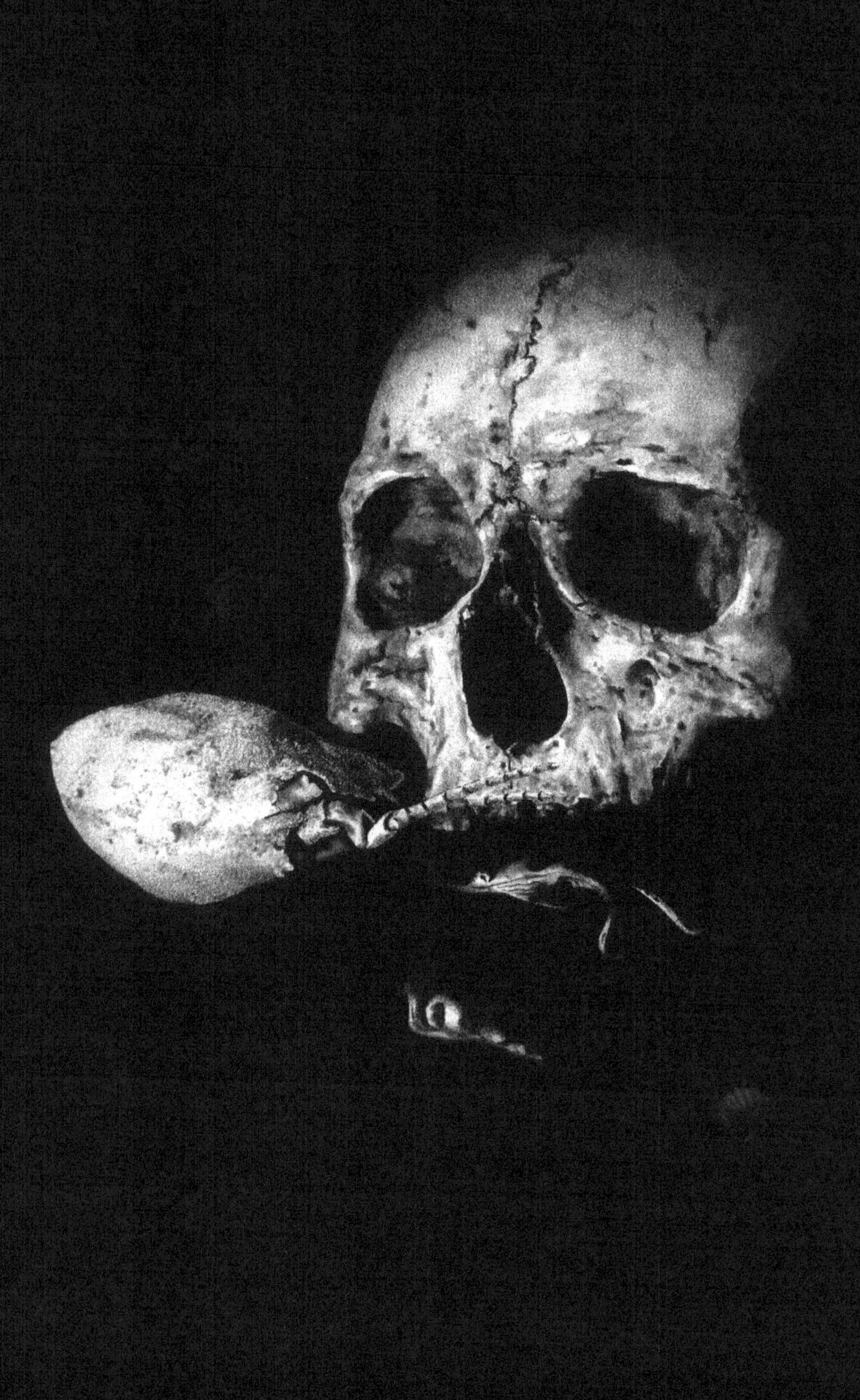

Lost at Sea

The storm came out of nowhere. Marius clutched at the ship's wheel in a death grip, swearing as he turned the bow into another wave. They were coming too frequently, and he feared that his small ship's motor wouldn't be able to keep up with the sea's demands.

He saw the wave forming ahead of him and drove his ship onward, hoping to pass over it before it broke. He felt as if he were on the world's most dangerous roller coaster, climbing slowly, the anticipation building, knowing that what goes up...

His ship crested the wave and began barreling down the other side. Marius looked out of his ship's window onto a chasm of churning water. His grip failed him, and he was tossed astern, hitting his head on the wall and falling unconscious.

To his amazement, he awoke still afloat and in calm waters. It felt eerily quiet after the din of the storm. Marius reached up to check his head for fractures, but he seemed to still be in on piece. He stood up, unsteadily, and saw nothing but a thick, bright fog.

Marius checked his equipment to see where he was, but none of it seemed to be functioning. He sighed. Somewhere outside, off in the fog to starboard, someone was calling to him. "Marius..." came the singsong voice of a woman in the distance. Marius swayed, his head becoming heavy. He 'suddenly felt like he had to go somewhere... somewhere in the fog.

"Ahoy!" came a voice to port, drifting in through a crack in the window. "Anyone aboard, ahoy!"

Marius went on deck and spotted the dark outline of a ship. "Ahoy yourself!" he called back. "My GPS is fried from the storm. Can you lead me to shore?"

"I can take you where you need to go," the man responded.

Marius managed to get the engine started and followed the ship ahead of him for what seemed like hours, yet the brightness and density of the fog never wavered. *Concussion,* he thought. *I'm not registering time correctly.*

Eventually, the outline of land came into view, and soon after, a small wooden dock. "Tie-up where you can!" came the voice of his mysterious benefactor, and Marius did as he was told. He took his first few steps off the ship, his legs expecting the dock to move just as the sea did, and nearly fell over. He was caught by the arm by a bear of a man.

"Careful, now," the man said. "Get your land legs back under you."

"Thanks," Marius replied, noticing the familiar tone of the man's voice. "You're the one who lead me here, aren't you?"

The man nodded. "Nils is my name. I thought I'd better take a look over the waves after that last storm. There's always someone who doesn't heed the warning signs that needs collecting." He eyed Marius gravely, and then winked and smirked. "Don't fret, now. It happened to all of us, one way or another."

Marius shrugged, but cracked a smile. "I suppose. My name is Marius," he said, offering his hand.

They shook. "Now that the pleasantries are over, we should be on our way. It doesn't do to linger in the fog for long." Nils looked out into the thick clouds, as if he recognized something, and then shook his head. "Come," he said.

Nils walked ahead on the dock while Marius marveled at the array of boats tied to the simple wooden dock. Canoes, life rafts, even longboats decorated with Norse figureheads were dotted all the way to the shore, with more piled up on the rocky beach.

"Where did they all come from?" he asked, unwittingly.

"Oh, them? Most have been here for years, but they all come from the same place you did." Nils smiled at his confusion. "You'll see," he concluded.

The fog thinned as they marched up a stone pathway further inland, and Marius was oddly sad to see it go. They passed through a small fishing village, and the inhabitants all greeted Nils as an old friend. Something seemed odd to Marius. They were beyond the village when he finally sorted it out. "Why were there so few women back there?" he asked.

Nils scratched at his beard. "Weeeeeeeell, you could say that it's a product of the occupation," he said, quickly moving on. "We're not far from where we're headed, now. We'll get you cleaned up and taken care of."

They pushed through a thin forest and up a hillside. The fog continued to thin. Looking back, Marius could just make out the lights from the fishing village in the distance.

The path took them to a town nestled in a clearing in the trees. The townspeople all nodded in greeting or said hello to Nils as he passed, and he replied to each greeting warmly. "You're quite popular," Marius said as they wove their way toward a large building in the center of town.

"That I am," Nils replied. "It's my natural charm." He started chuckling at his private joke. Marius rolled his eyes.

They entered a great wooden building, where they were met by a small crowd. The entire construction seemed to be one massive room, with a ceiling so tall that it disappeared into shadow above their heads. Marius blinked at the odd mix of people – some men in leather jerkins, others in t-shirts and jeans, and still more in old military uniform, bleached and torn, but recognizable. They all stopped their conversations as Nils entered the room.

"Only one today," he said, to the general nodding of those around him. "I think there may have been more, but with the fog..." he let the sentence trail off.

"A fine catch," one of the men called out.

"I wouldn't have gotten the one," called another.

An old man, bent with age and dressed in colorful robes came forward and held his hand out to Marius. "Welcome," he said. "We'll sort out a place for you to stay in a few days. In the meantime, you can bunk with any of these men."

Marius shook his head. "I'm sorry, there must be some confusion. I can't stay. I just need some repairs to my ship and then I can make my way home."

The old man turned to Nils. "You bastard," he said, his face growing dark. "You never have the heart to tell them, do you? Never do the hard part yourself!"

Nils rolled his eyes. "Isn't going and fetching them hard

enough?" he retorted.

"It isn't and you know it isn't!"

"Whoa, hold on," Marius interrupted. "Would someone tell me what's going on, here? What didn't anyone tell me?"

The old man glared at Nils, who sighed, defeated, and turned to Marius. "You came here on your ship, right?" he asked.

Marius nodded.

"Okay. Well, I saw that ship, and I can tell you that it's an awful lot for one man to handle. I would expect at least three or four men aboard. So, tell me, where is your crew?"

Marius thought for a few moments. The memory seemed to fight him all the way, but finally he remembered. "They were on deck when the storm hit. One... one was washed overboard, but the other made it back in. When I got knocked out, he was... below making sure the engine didn't go out on us."

"But he wasn't there when you came to, was he?"

"No... I guess he could have taken a lifeboat, but-"

"And left you behind? Bleeding on the deck? Was he that sort of a man?"

Marius shook his head. "Where did he go?" he asked.

Nils rubbed at his temples. "I'd wager he died, lad. Just shortly after you did."

Marius smiled. "Oh, right, great joke," he started, and then he looked at the faces around the room. Nobody was smiling. "But, I mean... I don't-"

"You hit your head, lad. You hit it hard, and it killed you," Nils said, quietly.

"If that's true, if I'm dead, then why isn't my crew here with me? Where are they?"

The old man patted him on the back. "As near as we can tell, the ones who drown go elsewhere. We all know that the sea is a jealous, greedy creature. We assume she simply doesn't let them go once she has them."

"You died before you went under," Nils interjected. "That's why you were there when I came looking."

Marius ran his hand through his hair. Something outside, far out at sea was calling to him, barely on the edge of hearing. He knew that he must choose, now, and live with the consequences. "No," he whispered, turning away and running outside.

The people in the town made no attempts to stop him as he ran past. They only looked on him with pity in their eyes. When Marius reached the edge of the forest, he gasped. The area surrounding the docks, visible now that the fog burned off, was covered with ships. Battleships from the world wars sat alongside wooden galleons, troop transports, private yachts, even Roman quinqueremes dotted the bay. He saw people moving along their decks, carrying on with their work.

Someone grabbed his arm and spun him around. Nils stood there, holding him in place. "Where do you think you will go?" he asked, turning him toward the sea once more. "Out there is oblivion. You were lucky that you didn't get sucked down and drowned the first time. Do you really think the sea will let you get away twice?" Nils let go of his arm and took a step back. "This is as good as it gets for us, lad. There's no going home, and there's only fools who try."

"I'm not going home! I have to know what she wanted, don't you understand? I have to go."

Nils' eyes went wide. "She can't be trusted. You'll wind up trapped in the deep with the others!"

Marius backed away. "I have to go," he said, and he ran. He reached the dock, climbed aboard his waiting ship, and started the engine. As he was pulling away, he saw Nils standing on the dock, watching him leave, unable or unwilling to stop him.

The further from land Marius went, the thicker the fog became. He could feel something out there, watching him, waiting. It wasn't long before he was hopelessly lost. After a time his engines quit, and he was adrift on the current. Somewhere in the fog, something called to him again, something sweet and promising. He had to know. He had to see it for himself.

"Marius..." came the woman's alluring call from the fog. "Come join us, Marius."

And he did.

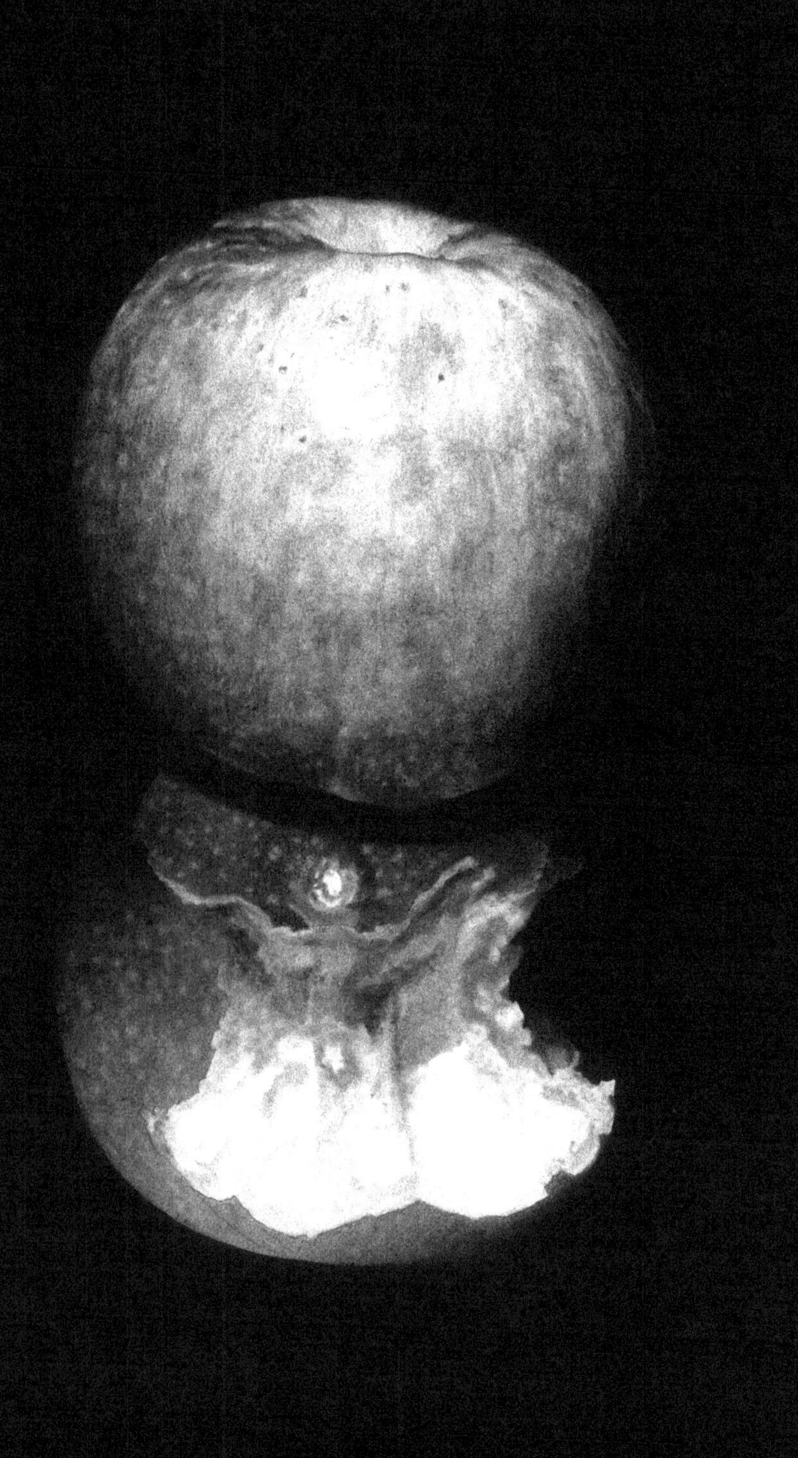

The Warmth of Illusion

Birthdays are an old kind of magic. We light candles, we make wishes to the wax of our past years, then we let them burn, blow them out, sending the smoke away with our wish to the ether, hoping it will be accepted. But it doesn't need to be so literal. Birthdays have a magic all their own.

Today was Xenia's birthday, but she had long ago stopped believing in magic. When the nights grew long and the warmth of day faded, she became more concerned with where her next scrap of food would come from, or if she would eat that day at all.

The frost had come on quickly that year, and she had found herself without enough layers of clothing and too few friends. She shivered under a torn, discarded shipping blanket and wondered if any of the warming shelters were open tonight, or if she could, possibly, beg enough money for a hot cup of tea.

Someone walking down the sidewalk cleared their throat, but

Xenia paid them no mind. Many people expected her to flee like a scared rat at the slightest provocation, but she stayed out of the way, here. The businesses were all closed at this hour, and she was always long gone by the time they opened in the morning.

A pleasant, if slightly gruff, voice spoke from the sidewalk. "Is that a dog under that pile of garbage? or is this a person I've found?"

Xenia looked up. A man stood before her wearing expensive shoes, dark slacks, and a large fur coat. He was just beginning to prepare a cigar – biting off the end and searching his numerous pockets for a lighter.

"Woof," Xenia replied, then huddled back down.

The man's laughter, she was sure, could be heard a mile away. "I must admit, I didn't expect you to have a sense of humor. So many of you lose that quality over time," he said, still searching for a lighter.

"What do you mean, 'so many of you'?"

"Vagrants, of course. Or is it 'the needy' these days? It's no longer acceptable to call you vagabonds, I know that much."

It was true. Xenia had never been called a vagabond. The man gave up his incessant patting of his pockets and looked down at Xenia like he had just been caught stealing from a church collection plate. "I, uh... I don't suppose..."

Xenia rolled her eyes, producing a simple plastic lighter. She held it up as he bent down to light his cigar. As he held it in the flame, she spoke. "Now who's needy?" she said, putting the lighter away.

The man smiled, blowing a ring of smoke into the air. "And you still have some fight in you? Remarkable."

"Live my life for a month. Having some fight in you helps keep you alive."

"Indeed," the man said, nodding. "Such is life. I bet you've never lost something you've really wanted without a fight."

Xenia shrugged.

"So, how did you end up out here, then?" the man continued.

"I fought. I didn't claim to always win," Xenia replied.

The man stood there for an uncomfortable length of time, smoking his cigar, looking her over. He pulled the cigar from his mouth and flicked it, sending a bright cascade of sparks out on the wind. "I may have a proposition for you," he said, finally, seemingly addressing the cigar.

"I don't do that," Xenia replied, quickly.

The man burst into laughter once again. "Oh, no, not that. If sex is what I were after, this would be an entirely different conversation."

"What, then?"

"What if I were to give you food, clothing, an apartment, amenitics, and other various necessities for... say, a year?"

Xenia raised an eyebrow at the man. "Are you mental?" she asked.

The man smiled. "I'm completely in earnest. Would that be worth something to you?"

Xenia thought of all the ways this could blow up in her face, if she might end up abducted, sold into slavery, killed – and then she thought of the cold nights ahead. "Okay, I'll bite. What's the catch? What do you want?"

He inhaled on his cigar until the embers lit up his face in a deep, orange glow, then blew out a thick cloud of noxious smoke. "Maybe I'm just generous," he said, smiling with the cigar in his teeth.

"Bullshit. Nobody is that generous."

The man laughed once more, coughing on the smoke in his

mouth. "True, true. Alright, I'll tell you." He knelt down in front of Xenia, his long coat dragging on the pavement. "I require something of yours. Something you don't even know you have, and something you will never miss."

Xenia stared at the man, waiting for him to continue, getting more annoyed by the second.

The man smiled. "It's a fair trade, don't you think?"

Xenia shook her head. "You haven't told me what you want, yet."

"Haven't I? Then let me be blunt: all I require of yours, is a wish."

"A wish?" Xenia scoffed. "What is it they call you rich madmen? Eccentric, isn't it?"

The man stood up and shook his head. "I'm serious, Xenia. On your next birthday, all I require is the use of your wish."

"Who told you my name?"

"Does it matter?" He took the cigar from his mouth and, without so much as flinching, put it out by grinding it into his own palm. "Now, I'm growing impatient. Last chance. Do we have a deal?"

Xenia thought for a moment. She didn't trust this strange man, but she also didn't enjoy feeling like she owed anyone for anything. Then the wind blew, sending a shiver down her spine. The man smiled and held out his hand to her. She looked at it, looked at her torn shipping blanket, and then took his hand.

The apartment, it turned out, was a small studio a few blocks from where they had met. The man opened a closet tucked behind an old Murphy bed. It was lined with various clothes in different styles and sizes. "Take what you want and get rid of the rest," he commanded.

When she asked about food, he reached into one of his various pockets and produced a credit card. The name on it was Lorien, and it was from a bank she'd never heard of. She said as much to the man. "No, I suppose you wouldn't have, but it will be accepted anywhere. No computer will dare refuse it, and no cash machine, either. The pin number is your name."

Xenia held the card tightly, as if it were a lifeline back to a familiar ship she never thought she'd see again. "Speaking of names, what's yours?" she asked.

"You can call me Nos," he said. Xenia noticed he did not claim it was his name. "Any other questions?"

"How do I get ahold of you? You know, if there's any problem, or the landlord comes knocking?"

"You don't." He smiled at her, nodded his head slightly, then headed for the door. "I'll see you in a year," he said. And then he was gone, and Xenia was alone.

The very first thing Xenia did was take a bath. It had been so, so long since she'd had a bath. She luxuriated in the water and suds. After, she went through the closet behind the bed, trying on this and that, separating them into piles of what she wanted and what she didn't. She got dressed in a sensible outfit of jeans and a sweater, keeping her own clothes folded on a chair in case this was all some sort of cruel joke.

She spent several long minutes staring at the credit card on the end table before she decided to try it out. She called a local pizza parlor and ordered something delivered to her. When they asked for the payment information, she gave them the numbers on the card. Then, she held her breath, expecting the worst. She didn't relax until the pizza was delivered. She ate it slowly, savoring it, waiting for the other shoe to drop.

But it never came.

She went to bed. As she covered herself in the thick, heavy blankets, she wondered how she could be so lucky. She ignored the tiny voice in the back of her mind screaming for attention, telling her that something was wrong. That night, she slept as if she hadn't slept in years.

Xenia lived the next few weeks like she was going to be caught stealing. She bought necessities, but only cheap ones, trying her best not to spend too much. As time went on, "too much" became a greater number, but it was never unreasonable. She never bought what she didn't need, and she never wasted anything if she could help it.

One night, a few months after meeting Nos, Xenia was walking home from the store. She wondered, vaguely, when she began to think of the apartment as home, and she smiled to herself.

Sitting on her building's stairs was a young woman, no older than Xenia herself. She looked at Xenia, and Xenia recognized the expression. She'd used it a thousand times before. It was a pleading in the eyes, a sadness in her dark face, saying *Please, don't make me move on.*

Xenia stopped and sat next to the woman, setting her groceries down. The young woman looked at her in confusion. "Still a bit cold at night these days, isn't it?" Xenia asked, staring at her feet.

The woman nodded, slowly.

"You know, I had to sleep with the window open for the first month that I had a place. I still can't sleep without fans blowing at me." She turned to the woman. "How long has it been since you slept indoors?"

"A while," the woman said. "Never could get used to it."

Xenia nodded. "You hungry?"

The woman smiled. "Always," she said.

"Great. Come with me, then." Xenia grabbed her bags and headed inside. "We can leave the windows open."

They went up to Xenia's apartment. The young woman stood in the doorway, peering in while Xenia set her bags down. She invited the woman in, told her to feel free to use the shower, have a nap, whatever she pleased, then set off to make dinner.

It was only after dinner that the young woman spoke. "How did you get all of this?" she asked.

Xenia shrugged. "There was this man, and he made me an offer. He said that-"

The young woman's eyes widened. "You made the deal, didn't you?" she breathed.

Xenia blinked. "Wait, you know about him?" she asked.

The woman nodded. "What did he get you for? Your favorite color? Your sense of justice?"

"What? No. All he asked for was a birthday wish."

"Girl," the woman said, accusingly, "you should know when things are too good to be true."

"What is it? What's wrong with a stupid wish in exchange for all of this?" But her companion only shook her head in response.

"How long have you got before he comes to collect?"

"Nine months or so," Xenia replied.

The woman stood up. "In that case, enjoy it while it lasts." She turned and walked out the door, leaving Xenia behind in the small studio apartment.

Xenia's stress rose with each passing week. She had spent months trying to track down the young woman who seemed to know so much about Nos and his dealings, but none of her friends on the streets knew who she was, and few ever saw her.

Autumn had come once again, and as the days grew shorter, so did her patience. She kept traveling further and further from her local area, returning to the apartment less and less. Sleeping rough was easier, she found, when she knew she had the option of a warm bed and a full stomach. But she had to know what the woman knew, had to find her.

It was after returning from a week-long expedition to the south side that she finally saw Nos again.

He was standing in her apartment when she walked in, smoking another of his horrendous cigars while he waited. He turned to her and smiled. "I was beginning to get worried," he said, billowing smoke. "When you hadn't been home for a week nor been using your card, I thought the worst had happened."

"I'm sure." Xenia's voice was cold. "What do you want?"

"Is that any way to treat your benefactor?" He shook his head and tsk'd. "Manners these days."

"Why didn't you tell me the full story?" Xenia stared at Nos, unblinking.

"But I did, child. I told you that you would get all of this for a year, and in exchange, I get your wish. What more did you need to know?"

"Then why are people treating me like I just sold my soul?"

Nos held the cigar halfway to his lips and turned to Xenia. "Who have you been talking to?" he asked.

Xenia balked. "I'm not telling you anything until you explain to me why this is so important to you."

Nos made a waving gesture with his hand. "I'm just a nice guy, alright?"

A voice came from the doorway. "No, you're really not."

Nos winced at the voice. "Ah, I see." He sighed. "Hello, mother."

Xenia turned to the woman in the doorway, the same woman she had been searching for. "Mother?" she asked.

The woman shrugged. "It's complicated."

Nos rolled his eyes. "No it isn't, you just don't age."

"You only say that because I never have."

"What is this about?" Xenia interrupted.

They both looked at her. Nos shrugged. "It's about wishes, and dreams, and you," he said.

His mother sighed. "He's been at this for centuries. Every time he comes across a human in dire straits, he pounces. And once he has his claws in..."

Xenia looked at the woman, her dark hair woven together in an intricate pattern, her eyes almost yellow. "Why did he need my wish?"

The woman smiled and turned to Nos. She looked at him, lovingly, as she spoke. "He just doesn't have the capacity to do all of this himself. He can make dreams, control sleep, but he can't experience them, himself. So, every once in a while, he gets a human to wish him into a dream of his own."

Nos shuffled his feet on the wooden floor, seeming smaller, somehow. "It's really not a bad deal, you know. I mean, you did get an extra year, just like I said. Does it matter if that year was only a dream?"

"This is a dream?" Xenia looked about the room, taking it all in. "No, this is real. This is life!"

Nos's mother smiled and shook her head. "You've been asleep since before you met Nos."

"I've been asleep for almost a year?

Nos laughed. "No, of course not. An hour, at best. But to you, it certainly felt like a year, didn't it?"

"So... I'm still out there? In the cold?! With nothing but a shipping blanket to-" The implication dawned on her all at once. "I'm going to die."

Nos nodded. "Not too much longer, now."

Well wake me up! I've got to get warm, find shelter, something!"

"It's too late for that, now. It was too late before we even began," Nos explained. "*People in dire straits*, remember?"

Xenia stared at him. "So what do I do, now?"

Nos's mother stepped forward and put her arm around Xenia's shoulders. "You've got a couple weeks left, dear. It's your dream. You can do whatever you damn well please," she said, and smiled. "Nos won't interfere anymore, will you, Nos?"

Nos shook his head. "It wouldn't work now, anyway. Can't control a conscious mind," he said, shifting his cigar to the other side of his mouth. "Anything you want, anything at all. It's your time. Use it wisely."

He stepped out of the room, and Xenia was suddenly sure that he was gone from her world for good.

The young woman hugged her. "Have a blast," she said, then left as well.

So Xenia was alone in her dream. She looked around the small studio apartment. "Complete control," she said to herself, flexing her fingers. "For the next few weeks, at least." And she took advantage of every second of it.

The next day, the coroner patiently verified that this young woman was dead. The passerby who called about the body was hanging back, morbidly curious. "Why is she smiling?" he asked.

The coroner shrugged. "The cold takes them like that, sometimes," he said.

55

Hunted

"How long do you think it will take you to come up with the money?" the man asked, straightening his tie, oozing pleasantness and camaraderie like a used car salesman.

"I don't know, Mr. Chance. After the shop was forced to close, and with jobs being scarce in these parts..."

Mr. Chance nodded. He knew the story. They had told it to him three times today already, every time he asked a direct question about the status of the owed funds.

The debtor who currently leased this flat from Mr. Chance's firm (his name had eroded with Mr. Chance's patience) continued to give his apologies and his excuses while fidgeting with an empty coffee cup. Mr. Chance ignored him, instead looking at his own. The bitter brew, cold now for an hour or more, sat undisturbed, the milk he had added out of habit forming a circle of white film in the center. He wondered if he should drink it now, if only for the look of the thing, but decided accepting even this small bit of gracious hosting would only give the debtor the wrong impression.

Instead, he looked around the room. He sneered internally at the commonplace furniture and low-cost food items visible on the kitchen counters. *Why does this town always smell of mold?* he thought, sniffing the air and stifling a cough.

Something in the conversation caught his attention. "I'm sorry, what was that?" he asked.

"I said – that is, I wanted to know if we could have a two-month deferment on the rent, just until we can sell off the old inventory and I can find a job."

Mr. Chance's plastic smile froze in place. "What kind of guarantee could we expect to receive for this generous extension?" he asked, already knowing the answer.

"I... I don't know," the debtor breathed, defeated.

Mr. Chance closed his eyes and nodded, solemnly. He formed what he thought of as a pitiable frown and looked at the debtor. "I'm afraid we can't do that sort of thing," Mr. Chance lied. "Not without collateral. If we did it for you, we would have to do it for everyone who asked, and then where would we be?" He stood up from the kitchen table and gathered his papers and copies of contracts into a leather satchel. "You and your family have the agreed upon fourteen days left to vacate the premises."

He turned to leave, but paused when he caught sight of two children standing in the living room. He replaced his plastic smile and grinned at them, halfway bowing as they looked on. Then he opened the door, and left.

The wind blew in from the north, bringing with it the scent of the sea and a promise of the coming storm. Mr. Chance turned his collar up and clasped his coat closed as he walked downhill toward the swing bridge and, eventually, to his hotel on the other side. A crescent moon peeked down at him through the clouds as he marched along. He cursed under his breath at the cobblestones that tripped him outside a local pub. The scent of stout beer and the ghosts of past roll-ups greeted him like an old friend, enticing him to enter, but he growled and stomped on.

The wind picked up and howled down the yards and walkways, through his too-thin coat and to his very soul. He shivered in the darkness. The streets were deserted, his lonely footsteps his only company. He made his way down thin streets and listened to the echoes of his breathing in the darkened shop windows as he passed.

Finally the street opened up, and there below him lay the swing bridge, shrouded in a thin mist from the inlet it spanned. The wind, so fierce further up the hill, was oddly still down here, but Mr. Chance paid it no mind. He smiled at the prospect of a warm shower that awaited him on the other side, the possibility of food and, perhaps, some company for the evening. The air was colder and completely calm near to the water. The mist deadened all sound, making his footsteps seem as if they were coming from another world altogether, and even the slip of moon seemed to abandon him as he started his way across.

He shivered. Nearby, he thought he heard something odd – a low, rolling, chilling sound that made his stomach lurch with ancestral dread. Humanity had known that sound since the dawn of the species, and had learned long ago to flee from it.

Mr. Chance raced across the bridge and down a nearby street toward his hotel. The mist began to thin. Here and there, in the lit windows above his head, he saw the unmistakable presence of humanity. Feeling foolish, he slowed to a walk once more, glancing over his shoulder to make sure nobody had noticed his moment of panic. There, shrouded in the mist, something waited.

He couldn't quite make it out – a snarl of fur here, a massive paw there – but he was absolutely sure it was watching him.

Fear stole his tongue as well as his legs, and he stood there motionless, staring at the creature who stared back at him. An unwelcome and unfamiliar thought came to his mind: *You are weak. You are pathetic. You are prey.*

The wind blew once more, blowing a bit of sand into Mr. Chance's eyes. He quickly rubbed at them to clear his vision, but when he could see once more, the creature was gone. Forgetting all pretense of dignity or embarrassment, he turned and ran to his hotel. He ran through the door to the common area, down the hallway, through the door to his room, and bolted it behind him. He took several deep, unsteady breaths, leaning on the closed door, sweating despite the cold.

His window was open, and he rushed across the room to close it. Blowing on the wind, he thought he heard a snarl that he hoped were just boats grinding against the quayside. He slammed the window shut, and a thought intruded on his reality once again. *Be better, Prey.*

The next day, Mr. Chance took a cab from the hotel to the train station, and from there he began to breathe easier as the scent of saltwater faded into the distance. By the time he reached his hometown, he had made up his mind that nothing out of the ordinary had happened the previous night.

Years passed. Mr. Chance progressed in his career with his firm, outperforming his coworkers year after year in profits and acquisitions. Finally he was promoted to run his own branch of the company. He was offered a position on the north coast, but he begged and pleaded with those in power and got a position further inland, instead. Months went by, and he exceeded the expectations of the board in every way imaginable.

One day, he received a call from the branch at the coast – the manager there had taken ill, suddenly, and he was needed to cover the day-to-day operations until she was back on her feet. Try as he might, he could do nothing to escape the assignment; either he went, or he would be finding a new job. And the next weekend, his heart in his throat, he took the train back to the northern coast.

To his pleasant surprise, the days passed without incident, though he always made damn sure to be back in his room before the sun set. His final day covering the branch was drawing to a close. He had spent fourteen days in the coastal town without so much as a minor headache, and he was looking forward to the train ride home in the morning. He closed and locked the office behind him, dropped the keys through the mail-slot as he was asked to do, then began the now familiar walk to his hotel.

The sun wasn't yet low in the sky, and the day was warm and pleasant for fall, so he took another route. He strolled along the old streets and glanced in shop windows, playing tourist as much as he was able. Finally he walked by a small pub. *Well, why not?* he thought, and went in.

He sat himself in an uncomfortable corner with a cool pint and took-in the local color, silently judging people whom he considered too-far gone from all that was real and immediate in his world. With the second pint, he found himself beginning to laugh at conversations in which he wasn't involved. By his fourth pint, he was arguing politics with two elderly locals. His seventh pint found him alone once more, grinning at the suddenly charming and comfortable surroundings. He hadn't realized how much stress he had really been under, and he sighed happily with the knowledge that tomorrow it would all be over.

"Hello, Mr. Chance," a familiar voice interrupted.

Mr. Chance turned. There, smiling wide, stood the same man who had pleaded with him years before about the rent. "Uh..." Mr. Chance stammered.

"Enjoying yourself?" the man asked.

Mr. Chance struggled to remember the man's name, but the information was swimming against the flow of beer, and he simply couldn't.

"Yes, in fact," replied Mr. Chance, regaining what he thought of as his professional demeanor, the whole effect ruined by him spilling the remains of his pint on the table as he straightened.

The man was undisturbed. "I'm very glad to hear that. I always like to hear when patrons are enjoying themselves in my pub."

Mr. Chance froze. "Your pub?"

"Oh, yes. After you and your firm kicked my family out on the streets, the former owner gave us a place upstairs to stay. To pay him back for his generosity, I took up tending his bar. As it turns out, I'm quite an able host and bartender, and upon the owner's death, he left this place to me." There was a deadly joy in his voice.

Mr. Chance cleared his throat. "Well, uh... congratulations. It is a wonderful pub. Very nice... walls. Now, if you'll excuse me, I'm just going to pay my tab and go." He stood up, but the owner moved into his path.

"Pay your tab? Why, Mr. Chance, you once didn't think I was worthy of lending money to, and now you're running tabs at my pub? Tell me, did you give any collateral for your drinks?"

"What? No, I–"

"Of course not, Mr. Chance. I think I don't want your money. In fact, I don't think I'll ever want your money, nor you, in my establishment ever again." He stood aside and held an arm out toward the door, still smiling. "Good evening, Mr. Chance, and goodbye," he finished.

Mr. Chance pretended he didn't see the bemused faces of the other patrons in the bar as he walked out the door, nor hear the following calls and insults. The door slammed behind him, and all he could hear was uproarious laughter from within.

He kicked the stone wall of the building as he passed and swore under his breath. He was angry, and more than a little drunk, so he didn't notice when he began walking in the wrong direction. By the time he realized, it was too late. The sun was setting.

He wandered in what he could only assume was the right direction, turning this way and that through the city's winding streets. Eventually, he came to a small turn and a sign that said, simply, Arguments Yard. He leaned against the wall, resolute that he would ask the next person he saw for directions to his hotel. He sighed at the empty street, and continued on his way.

Turning a corner, he spotted something just up the road. It could only be a very large, very ragged dog, black and strong and long-haired, and it was watching him. He saw the familiar sign of his hotel directly behind the beast, as if it knew – as if it was waiting for him.

Mr. Chance backed away slowly, turning the corner once more before bursting into a sprint. He had his bearings, now, and knew his way back to the office. Surely he could find a place in there to rest. He could lock the door behind him, and–

The keys!

He remembered, now. He would find no shelter there. Quickly

ducking into a yard, he stopped running. Slowly, he peered around the corner, back the way he had come.

The street was deserted.

The Pub, he thought, *I'll just go back there and beg his forgiveness, offer him a fortune for his troubles, if only he'll take me in for the night. Surely he wouldn't turn me down.*

He turned to continue on his way and nearly ran into the beast that sat there, falling back onto the cobbles. The creature cocked its head at Mr. Chance, as if it were perplexed, or amused. Even seated, the beast stood more than a head taller than Mr. Chance, and he wondered if the beer had gotten to his senses. The beast, calm and controlled, closed its yellow eyes and sniffed at the air, following the scent, moving closer to Mr. Chance's face, inhaling his breath with one, long drag.

Its eyes snapped open, and Mr. Chance felt more naked than if his essence were ground, strained, filtered, and examined by a panel of angry gods. *Prey,* came the unbidden thought, and the creature seemed to grow ever larger with each breath it stole from Mr. Chance's lungs. Its long, tangled fur bristled, and it growled, slow and deadly, like the death of light.

Mr. Chance scrambled back on his hands and stood already in mid-run, headed deeper into the yard as the hound advanced on him with cruel and inevitable intent. He tried to scream, but his voice came out as a strangled squeak. He could feel the weight of the misery in his life, all of the pain, the fear, the anguish he had caused pulled him down like an anchor, and he fell, hard, on the cobblestones, and still he retreated. He turned, and the beast was upon him. His entire reality seemed to be filled with fur, and teeth, and the smell of decay.

The hound leapt, and Mr. Chance closed his eyes...

"Hey mister, are you okay?"

The voice was pleasant and young, and came from behind him.

"What?" he asked, keeping his eyes closed.

"I said, are you okay? Did you hurt yourself?"

Mr. Chance turned and saw a young woman standing in an open doorway, cigarette and lighter at the ready. "I..." He scrambled to his feet and darted his eyes in every direction. "Did you see it?" he asked.

"See what?"

"That creature! Did you see it!?!"

The young woman glared at him. "Maybe a few less pints next time, yeah?" she said, mumbling insults as she closed the door.

Mr. Chance was alone, and he ran. He ran out of the yard, he ran down the street, and as he ran he thought of his escape. *I can't go to my hotel, that thing knows where it is! How did that damn demon find me? How can I hide from it?*

He turned and found himself standing in front of a great series of steps. At the top, basking in the moonlight, he saw the outline of an old church. "Holy ground," he whispered, smiled to himself, and began to climb.

His legs ached, and on he climbed. His lungs threatened to burst, and on he climbed. He threw his legs upward and forward into the darkness, whether he saw the next step or not. He was seeing spots as he crested the last stair. He collapsed onto the ground, coughing and wheezing, gulping in the cool night air.

He looked up, saw the church, and a smile spread across his face. Holy ground – he had made it. He was safe. He was sure that he was safe.

The next morning, the people of Church Street were shocked to see the body of a man in a torn and tattered business suit lying at the base of the steps. One of them recognized him as a drunken fool who had been ranting at her the night before, and everyone soon concluded that, drunk and unbalanced, he had fallen to his death down all one-hundred-and-ninety-nine steps.

As for the strange cuts and gashes on his body – well, some of those steps are sharp, weren't they? And if anyone noticed the strands of black fur matted into his bloodied flesh, or the unmistakable scent of sulfur in the air, nobody said a single word about it.

67

Name Your Poison

There are places in the world unlike any other. Places that have exactly what it is you're looking for that day, that very moment, and it is always the perfect thing.

Sometimes these places are curio shops, with their random collection of oddities and hidden treasures, and sometimes they're cafés, serving local arts and crafts along with coffee, tea, and finger foods.

Silenus ran a pub, which he had named after himself as a matter of course. A man entered the dark, empty room right at sunset and took a place at the bar. Silenus smiled into a face not unlike a storm cloud. "Having a bad day?" he asked, jovially.

"A bad life is more like it," the man replied. "Gimme a beer."

Silenus cocked his head toward the man. "But you don't want a beer," he said, turning to a shelf full of dusty bottles behind him. He selected one, rubbed at the label, smiled, and uncorked it. "Now this... this is what you're looking for."

He poured the thin, red liquid into a metal goblet that he had produced from under the bar. The customer eyed the goblet, confused.

"It helps the flavor," Silenus encouraged.

"What is it?" the customer asked.

"Just an old Roman wine," Silenus said, corking the bottle once again. "Try it. I promise you'll enjoy it." The customer picked up the goblet carefully, sniffing at the contents. He made a face at Silenus, who only laughed. "Trust me," he said. "I'd hardly get anywhere poisoning my customers, now would I?"

The customer took a drink, and it was as if the wine had put out an inferno within him. His muscles un-knotted themselves, his jaw un-clenched, and the pain that had been a part of him for so long that he no longer remembered that it was there or where it had come from was suddenly gone. He looked at Silenus, his mouth agape. "That..." he paused, turning this way and that, looking for anyone who might overhear. "That tastes like... like summer. It tastes as good as sleep feels. It..." he took another sip. "It tastes like the innocence of childhood."

Silenus nodded . "Told you that you'd like it," he said, putting the bottle away.

The man pushed the drink away, his face suddenly full of panic. "There's no way I can afford something like this," he breathed.

Silenus laughed and pushed the goblet back toward the man. "You've already paid," he said, putting the cork on a small vial of cloudy, purple liquid. The man looked at the goblet, then up to Silenus, then carried the goblet to a nearby table. Silenus nodded at the man's back, then wrote *Despair* on a label and stuck it to the bottle.

The night carried on much the same way. The usual crowd of people looking for stout happiness shuffled in with the stranger people who always craved unfiltered sorrow. One woman wanted a high-proof rage, a middle-aged man wanted concentrated time, and an elderly gentleman surprised Silenus by knowing exactly what he wanted: a first kiss with water, to make it last.

It was getting toward closing, and the regulars were staggering out in various states of elation or horror. Silenus took inventory of his receipts for the night, admiring a particularly potent nightmare he had obtained from a rather strange man who had traded it for a tea made from an Egyptian mummy.

A woman walked in just as Silenus was about to lock the doors. "Are you closed?" she asked, sweetly.

"Madam, Silenus has never turned away anyone who was able to make it over the threshold." He ushered the woman in, but turned over the 'open' placard to show 'closed' to the outside world. He escorted her to a seat at the bar, then proceeded behind it as the woman looked around the empty room.

"If this is a bad time, I can come again tomorrow," she offered, but Silenus waved her off and shook his head.

"Nonsense. Why come back when you're already here? Now then, what can I get you?"

The woman looked along the rows upon rows of bottles – some new, some dusty and faded, and some chained down, gently rattling. She swore one was looking back at her. "I'm afraid I'm not sure," she replied.

Silenus smiled. "That's no problem, I can-" He stopped, tilting his head to one side. "No, I guess I can't, at that. You really don't know what you want, do you?"

"I did tell you as much." She sighed.

Silenus' smile widened. "Dear lady, you have no idea what a distinct pleasure it is to meet someone who truly doesn't know what they want." He excitedly began to grab bottles and concoctions, spirits both real and imagined, and pile them all on his work area. "Now, I really get to show you my skill."

His hands moved with inhuman speed over the assembled ingredients, taking a short-pour of one, a drop of another, tipping them all into a thin metal shaker. He used a pair of long pliers to take a distorted and twisted bottle full of black liquid down from a shelf above his head. He set the bottle, unopened, next to the shaker.

After several seconds, he grabbed the shaker, tossed a small, cold stone into it, slammed a pint glass on top to seal it, and started shaking. He counted aloud to seven, and then cracked open the shaker and poured the strangely green and blue striped substance into a martini glass. He tore a sprig of rosemary from a collection of plants nearby and laid it in the glass before presenting it to the woman.

She looked at it, unsure, then looked to Silenus, silently questioning.

"It's something I haven't made in years. One of my old pupils used to absolutely love it."

"What is it called?" she asked, looking at the color swirling together and coming apart in the glass.

"Ambrosia."

The woman lifted the glass to her lips and sipped at it. It tasted like unpracticed love – sweet and pleasant as it entered her mouth, but turning almost foul as the flavor lingered. She sat the glass down once again. "It's good, but not quite what I was looking for," she said.

Silenus was stunned. He hadn't had a reaction like that to one of his drinks in eons, but he soon regained his composure and shrugged. "It's not for everyone." He stroked his thin beard for a moment, then snapped his fingers and set to work on another mixture.

He moved this way and that, mixing one ingredient into another, pouring that into a larger glass, then stirring it. He took a vegetable peeler and shaved a piece of cloud he kept in a jar in the fridge, then piled spices on top of it, sinking the cloud to the bottom of the glass. The finished drink was perfectly clear and seemed to glow from within. He transferred it to a highball glass and put a silver bendy-straw into it.

The woman sipped on the straw and immediately made a face. "And what do you call this?" she asked, pushing it away.

Silenus sighed. "Life, and you have my condolences." He shook his head. "Perhaps you're in the mood for something a little darker?"

The woman shrugged, folding her hands together and resting her chin upon them, her elbows on the bar.

She sat in that barstool for hours, watching him create one strange concoction after another – a froth of tea from the leaves of Yggdrasil, beer from the court of Tutankhamun mixed with the souls of murderers, spiced wine from the gardens of Babylon, condensed sex thinned with the blood of Julius Caesar – and each time, she was unsatisfied.

Growing desperate, Silenus broke into his special stock: apple cider from the tree of knowledge, heated with magma from Vesuvius, a banana shake topped with the tears of Eric the Red, a double shot of pure, unrestricted lust, and an odd combination of things that seemed to scream to her very soul as she drank that he called The Past that Never Was. Still she sat there, perched on her stool, unmoved in body or spirit.

Silenus shook his head. "The only other drinks I have are deadly poisonous to humans, I'm afraid."

She lifted an eyebrow. "Really? That would be interesting. Give me one of those," she said.

Silenus stared at the woman. "Miss, I really do mean it. Five seconds, maybe ten, and you'll no longer be among the living. Is that really something you want?"

"We'll see, won't we?"

Silenus hesitated for just a moment. He had never refused a customer before, not for anything. But then, he'd never been asked to kill one, either. He sighed.

"As you wish," he said, and went to work.

He started with a base of cyanide, delightful to smell, but bitter to taste. He added a mixture of guava and honey into it. From there, he muddled some mint and asp venom together with limes, then topped it with a shot of moonshine. Finally, he stepped back into the racks and shelves behind the bar and grabbed a small vial. He returned and unsealed the wax from around the cork, punctured the top with a needle, and turned it upside down. A single drop of a thick, dark substance slipped from the needle and into the mixture. "What's that?" the woman asked.

Silenus huffed. "Madam," he said, "that's Death." He smiled at her oddly curious expression. He poured the murky mixture into a pint glass rimmed in arsenic powder, then added a lime wedge to the rim. He stepped back and looked at it, then he snapped his fingers and added the carapace of a black widow to the liquid and watched it sink to the bottom of the glass. He slid the drink over to the woman, stepped back, and waited.

The woman stirred the drink with her finger, knocking the lime into the glass. She wiped her finger on her pants, picked up the glass, and drank.

She paused for a moment, licked her lips, then turned to Silenus. She opened her mouth to speak, and then fell backward off of her stool.

Silenus rubbed at his temples with his hands, wondering how to get rid of a body at this time of night, and who might owe him that kind of favor.

He went around the bar to collect the body and looked down at the woman with pity. "I did warn you," he said.

The body blinked once, twice, and then sat up. "My compliments," the woman said. "I think that was exactly what I needed." She smiled at Silenus. "It's funny," she continued as her hair began to grey and fall from her head. "I had come here for completely different reasons. I was going about my business, you know? Night is always a busy time for me."

She stood up and brushed off her pants. The skin from her hands stayed on the cloth, and she sighed. "Maybe I should take breaks more often. It really has been so very long." The flesh dripped down her face like candle wax, pooling on her shirt collar. Her eyes receded into her head, and all that was left was a grinning skull. She held out a skeletal hand, and, as Silenus shook it, with the same sweet voice, she thanked him for his time. "You really are a wonderful host," she added. Then she turned away, and walked out the door.

Silenus stood there for a moment, dumbfounded, as he watched the bits of skin and blood on his floor evaporate in streams of smoke. He locked the door behind his guest, then went behind the bar to collect his payment. He put a cork in the bottle of shimmering, shifting grey liquid, then wrote on a small label *Death's Indecision* and put it on the shelf, wondering what new drinks he could make with that.

<u>To Spite the Living</u>

It was an unseasonably warm day in the north of England. People flocked to the streets and stores in t-shirts and trousers. Some of them put on their spring dresses even though it was only February, and moved about the crowds like spots of light in a grey world. The churchyard, by contrast, was quiet and calm.

William had always loved old churchyards. It was something about the look – desolation kept with care – that struck a chord with him. All across the United Kingdom, he had visited old churchyards and ruins, sat in them a while, explored the grounds, and, if at all possible, took souvenirs home with him.

He was not a grave robber. At least, he never thought of himself as one, although he had collected the odd bit of bone or piece of statue from time to time while on his adventures. A finger joint here, a bit of rib there, things so small as to not be missed unless you were looking for them. And if he had to pay the occasional caretaker a little extra for them, so be it. He was a collector, and hobbies cost money.

William paced back and forth along a row of ancient head-stones. The names, once cut so deeply into them, were now shallow and hard to read among the dried moss and lichen. His contact was late. He had been waiting for over an hour, trying to be as inconspicuous as possible, pacing, and was quickly getting fed up. He kicked at a stone in the grass and sent it flying into a tombstone, where it hit with a hollow, light sound. Curious, he over to it, looked around, then bent over to pick it up.

What he had kicked turned out not to be a rock at all, but an old, thin bit of bone. He inspected it closely, but try as he might, he couldn't identify its origin. Someone behind him coughed and he spun around while holding his new treasure out of sight. Sitting on a wide tomb a few rows back from the older graves sat a woman in a simple dress, her leg over her knee, smiling at him.

"I'd put it back if I were you," she said, no malice at all in her tone.

"Put what back?" William replied, playing dumb.

"Well, darling," the woman started, tilting her head to on side. "If you can't sort that out for yourself, then I really can't help you."

William stared at her for several seconds, trying his best not to show the rising panic he felt. The woman never stopped smiling at him, as if she were having a private joke. Finally, William cleared his throat. "I'm afraid you're mistaken. I have nothing," he said, then put the piece of bone in his pocket and walked away.

As he was passing through the churchyard gates, he thought he heard laughter from a long way off, but when he turned around, the woman was gone.

It was a several hour drive back to his home, and night had fallen by the time William stepped through his door. He took his new prize out of his pocket and placed it on the dining room table. Looking at it in the light, he wondered if it might be an animal bone of some kind.

"Look who's talking, ape," a voice called out.

William nearly jumped out of his skin. He ran through the house with a fire poker in his hand, trying to locate the intruder. He looked everywhere, but he was alone. He sat down at the table once again, sweating from fear and surprise, thinking he had imagined the voice he heard.

"You're not that clever," the voice announced.

"Who's there?" William shouted, poker at the ready. A deep, throaty laughter was all that replied. William sat in silence for several minutes, trying his best not to freak out. *Am I going mad?* he thought.

"You're already mad, Willy. You steal bones for fun, you daft bastard." The voice was confident, amused.

"How do you know my name?" William asked.

"It's all over your mail," replied the voice.

William swallowed in a dry throat. "Where are you?" he asked, his voice cracking.

"Oh, a game! It's been so long since I've had a game. Alright, you guess, and I'll tell you if you're warm or cold."

"What?"

"You want to know where I am? Those are my terms." William stood up, keeping his makeshift weapon with him, and peered into the kitchen. "Oh, cold, Willy. Ice cold. Antarctic!"

William growled under his breath. He hated being called Willy. He made his way down the hallway and toward his bedroom.

"You're on Pluto, now," the voice called out, but was no quieter. William went into the bathroom and used the poker to open the shower curtain. "Honestly, ape, it's like you're not even trying."

"This is a ridiculous game," William shouted.

"If you had asked me my name, we could be playing charades," the voice replied.

William rolled his eyes and went back to the dining room table. "This prank isn't funny," he announced.

"...Warmer," teased the voice.

William frowned, then peered under the table. The voice started laughing. "You're really bad at this," it said.

"Just tell me where you are, you bastard!"

The voice was silent for a moment, then said "I am exactly where you put me."

"Excuse me?"

"By all the veil, you are thick, aren't you? Honestly, Willy, no wonder you live alone."

William's eyes dropped to the table, and the piece of bone sitting there.

"By the gods! Realization finally dawns for the idiot," the voice teased, laughing.

William shook his head. "I'm calling the police," he said, getting out his cell phone.

"Oh, yes, that will go so very well. 'Hello? Police?'" the voice mocked. "'There's a bone I stole from a churchyard and it won't stop pointing out what an absolute git I am!' That's bound to work. I'll just wait for them to come and drag me away, shall I?"

William paused, then hung up the phone. "What do you want?"

The voice laughed in delight. "We get to play charades, after all!"

William sat, unmoved, and didn't reply.

"Awe, are we no longer playing, Willy?" the voice goaded.

"You might be, but I'm not. This is absurd."

"Says the man who collects cold calcium deposits. Obviously a fount of sanity, you are."

"A lot of people have hobbies!" William shouted at the bone fragment.

He couldn't see it, but William had the distinct impression that, should the bone fragment have had eyes, it would have rolled them. The voice sighed. "You're almost too easy," it said. "What game shall we play, now?"

"I told you," William replied. "I'm not playing."

"Are you a betting man, William?"

"What?"

"Do you gamble? Take chances? Risk losing something in order to gain something more?"

"What does that have to do with anything?" William growled.

"Look, when a sentient piece of bone that's sitting on your table asks you a question, you bloody well humor it. Got it?"

"I don't have to. This might not even be happening."

"Oh, you mean you might be asleep?" the voice asked, a dangerous edge to its tone.

"Yeah, or hallucinating, or something!" William sat back, exasperated.

There was silence for a moment, then "You're right," the voice said. "You might be dreaming. We should wake you up."

William woke up just as the his car went over the edge of the cliff, bursting through the guardrail without even slowing down. He was weightless, hitting his head on the roof of his car as he sailed downward toward the churning ocean and jagged, unforgiving rocks.

He screamed. He was back at his table once more. The voice was laughing. "Are you awake, now?" it asked, amused.

"That doesn't prove anything!" William shouted.

The voice sighed, and then William punched himself in the groin. He shouted in surprise at the altogether alien feeling of losing control of his own limb. Through the haze of pain, he heard the voice ask "And how about now? Still dreaming?"

"What the hell was that?!" William screamed.

"What?" William flung his own shin into the table leg. "That? Are you really that thick?"

"How are you doing that?"

"We possess certain powers, ape, even in death. Controlling weak-willed individuals is hardly a challenge."

"We?"

The voice chuckled. "Dragons," it said.

"Dragons don't exist," William said. His hand jumped up and grabbed hold of the top of his own ear.

"Do you know how much force it takes to remove a human ear?" the dragon asked. "Only a few pounds. Normally, the pain keeps you from even getting close to that point. Your body simply won't let you. However, since I can't feel it-"

William screamed as his ear slowly peeled away from his skull. He stared, helpless, at the lump of flesh pinched in fingers he could no longer control.

"Does it bounce, do you think?" asked the dragon as William involuntarily threw his detached ear at the table. "It does! Wonderful!"

"I need-" William breathed.

"To stop insulting the creature who is only keeping you alive for its own amusement? I agree."

He tried to stand, but his legs refused to obey.

He tried to reach out and throw the bone out of the window, but didn't even manage to lift his finger.

William swallowed in a dry throat, resigned to his fate. "What do you want?" he asked.

"Oh, Willy-boy... we're just getting started..."

A crash came from William's study. One by one, he watched as his treasured collection rolled, clattered, and crawled its way into the dining room. The bits and pieces of bone and stone combined together into a grotesque mockery of William, himself. The Collection moved forward and pulled him to his feet by his collar. In a thousand dead, hollow voices, it shrieked at him.

Suddenly it went dark, and William was surrounded with the stench of rotting meat, bile, and just a hint of sulphur. He managed to turn his head to see the shadow of enormous teeth clamp shut in front of his eyes, and he wept.

"Have you been naughty, sweetie?" asked a woman's voice from outside the darkness. William didn't know how long he'd been here, but the voice sounded oddly familiar.

"He started it," the dragon replied.

"Well, yes. But he's an idiot, whereas you are very wise. Isn't that how we came to our arrangement?"

The voice grumbled and growled. "That was a long time ago. Things change," it said.

The woman's tone was gentle and soothing. "Come back with me, darling. Leave this fool to his misery."

"I don't want to. I have plans for this one..."

"Don't make me banish you," the woman teased. The dragon growled.

"You got lucky the first time, witch," it said, but the fight was out of it.

"Maybe, but once was all it took."

William opened his eyes. He was sat at his table, his head down. He lifted his head and gasped as the scab on the side of his head peeled away, still stuck to the table. Across from him, holding the dragon bone fragment, sat the woman from the churchyard. She smiled at William. "I did warn you, dear," she said, sweetly.

"You... you did all of this, didn't you?!" William jumped up, pushing his chair to the floor, and was about to dive at the woman when he froze.

Gripped in the woman's other hand was the hilt of a sword which had a blade so impossibly thin as to be nearly unseen, the tip of which was pressed, lightly but assuredly, against William's throat.

"He really is a git, isn't he?" the woman asked.

"It's almost impressive," the dragon replied. "I'm keeping his ear, just so you know."

The woman withdrew and somehow hid the blade with a flick of her wrist. William staggered backward, falling over his own chair.

"Suits me," the woman said, smiling again. She tilted her head to one side. "Well, darling, maybe this will teach you a lesson. And I would get that wound looked at, if I were you." She leaned forward, putting her hand up to her mouth. "It's starting to smell," she whispered.

And with that, she turned and left.

The next day, William stood in the churchyard once again, a bandage wrapped around his head. He paced up and down the graves and tombs, one after the other, trying to make sense of everything that had happened, gibbering to himself about kidnappers and hidden speakers.

Unseen, a few graves over, a woman and dragon watched. The woman shook her head in disappointment, then scratched the dragon under the chin, shrugged at it, and smiled as they both faded into the mist.

Don't Look

The streets were a dangerous place, it seemed. Every day, Michael heard of a new mugging or robbery, a new rape or murder in the alleys and streets that he frequented. Looking around tonight, half-drunk and bemused, Michael wandered between the local bars.

He turned down a street and narrowly avoided running into a man who stood in the middle of the sidewalk. Instead, he sidestepped into a signpost. Michael picked himself up off the ground (with effort, his alcohol consumption finally making itself known) and turned toward the man he had almost ran down. He was about to scream at him, but something in the man's face made him pause.

The man wasn't looking at him. He was looking, unblinkingly, over Michael's shoulder. The stranger's eyes were red-rimmed, they twitched with the effort of remaining open, and they were absolutely filled with terror.

Curiosity getting the better of him, Michael tried to turn to see what the stranger was looking at.

Then the man's hand was around Michael's throat. The stranger pulled him close to his chest, the scent of his unwashed body filling Michael's senses. The man's chapped lips brushed against Michael's ear as he whispered in a half-maddened tone:

"Don't look behind you!"

Michael pried the stranger's hand from his throat and stepped away from him. "What the hell is wrong with you?!" he screamed. But, again, the stranger wasn't looking at him.

"Don't worry. You aren't in any danger–not yet, at least. You'll be fine. Just, for the love of all that you hold dear, don't look behind you."

Michael paused, looking-over the stranger. His eyes were fixed, his jaw was set–he was serious. Michael swiveled his eyes to look to his side, trying to catch sight of whatever was behind him in his periphery, but it was no use. He stood there for several moments, unsure of what to do. *If I move, he'll attack me again. But what's to stop him if I stay?* He tried once more to turn his head. At the corner of his eye, he could have sworn he saw a strange, clawed arm... Then the stranger's hand turned Michael's head back once again. "Don't," he said, simply.

While Michael debated with himself, the stranger cleared his throat. He rubbed his stubbled chin with a dirty, scarred hand, and then began to speak as if he had been asked.

"I knew a boy once, and he was scared–scared of the dark, scared of loud noises, scared of small creatures and great. Most of all, he was scared of what was hiding under the bed.

"He knew, as only children know, that there was something *other* under the bed, patiently waiting for him to make a mistake. He dare not leave his feet uncovered, nor would he lay with his hands over the edge of the mattress, but what he couldn't resist was sleep. Oh how he struggled, struggled, struggled against sleep, for whenever he closed his eyes he would hear gentle breathing from beneath the bed like the ebb and flow of ocean waves.

"For months he dreaded the ritual of bedtime: hated brushing his teeth, despised his nightly bath, couldn't bear the words "Good night." Until, one night, perhaps driven mad by exhaustion or driven to bravery by soul-gripping terror, he decided he'd had enough. He was going to meet The Creature Under the Bed."

Michael was awe-struck. He was half-drunk, slightly bruised, and being told a bedtime story by a madman. And yet, he wanted to know more.

"The night was warm and comfortable. Streetlights illuminated his blinds, filling the room with a faint, gentle glow. The boy lay in his bed, nervous, excited, biding his time. He waited until his eyes adjusted to the gloom, and then began to breathe in a long, gentle rhythm. He struggled, at first, to maintain his pace–his excitement getting the best of him–but he refused to give up.

"Time passed. The boy's breathing slowed, his eyes closed, and at the very moment of Morpheus's triumph, a subtle noise emanated from under the bed: the slow hiss of The Creature. Scrapes and muffled echoes of movement greeted the boy, who dared not open his eyes. He heard it crawl out from the bed. The air moved around him and he felt the hair on his neck stand at attention. He lay limp while his mattress shifted with the weight of The Creature from Under the Bed as it stood on too-many limbs straddling the boy, trapping him in place.

"He felt its hot, stinging breath upon his cheek. Sharp shards of hair brushed against his face as it rhythmically sniffed the air.

"Suddenly, The Creature jumped off of the bed and landed on the floor with a thud. The boy threw off his blankets and searched for it, but only caught a glimpse of a claw-like leg as it vanished into the shadow below the bed. Regretfully, the boy gave chase.

"He rolled from his bed and belly-crawled after The Creature. Walls and warm carpet gave way to cold, damp stone, barely high enough to pass through, but he pressed on. He heard The Creature in the distance, its hands slapping against the stone, its legs scraping along and pushing it forward. It shrieked with a voice like cold steel. The boy was gaining on it, grasping at the darkness ahead of him.

"Finally, the air changed. The echo wasn't quite so close, the air was colder–there was open space around him. He listened intently for The Creature, but all he could hear was his own heartbeat pounding in his ears. Then, far above, a bright light shown over the edge of a great cliff. Blinking back tears, the boy realized that this was no cavern nor pit. It was a canyon, and he had emerged at the bottom of it. There, across the grey, stone canyon floor, something shuddered and began to take shape. By the light of the moon, the boy finally saw The Creature as it unfolded into its full height..."

Here, the stranger paused, and for the briefest of moments his eyes lost the ghastly stare that they held in perpetuity.

"My dear friend, there are things in existence that were never intended to be witnessed by the human eye. Things so alien, so bizarre, that the mind struggles to grasp for comparison. Failing comprehension, the witness slowly goes insane as the mind attempts to bury the memory of what it couldn't have seen by inventing lesser horrors. What I can tell you with certainty is that the boy saw a thing which was unafraid, and which seemed to smile at him.

"The boy left that place, but he did not hurry. He felt no fear of the darkness ahead as he blindly crawled through it, nor any trepidation of what it could contain. He held no terror of The Creature any longer, although he heard it scurrying close behind, patiently waiting when the boy sometimes lost his way. It no longer hid itself from the boy. It had no reason to.

"The boy crawled out from the darkness under his bed and, carefully, rolled between the covers. He didn't react when he felt something cold and clammy crawl into bed with him. He even took comfort from the soft hiss that filled the air and the gentle touch of The Creature as it stroked his hair with its ragged limbs.

"In the morning, the boy awoke alone. The Creature was nowhere to be seen. In a daze, unsure of what was real or nightmare, the boy went out into the dining room. His mother sat at the table eating a simple breakfast. She looked up, smiled at him, and said good morning, but the boy did not respond. He didn't even look at her. He was too busy looking behind her at the multi-jointed arm that went to a mouth, one of many, connected to a horror too real to exist.

"Quietly, it hissed 'Shhhhhh...'"

Michael watched the stranger's eyes. There, right in the pit of them, he thought he saw teeth flashing in the streetlight. The stranger swallowed in a dry throat, then continued.

"Time passed, but The Creature became the boy's constant companion, always out of sight to anyone but him. Try as he might, tell who he might, nobody believed his ramblings, his story about his journey beneath the bed, nor that he could see the creature.

"But now, my dear friend, I have told you. You can believe it or not, as you will. But, please, for your own sake..." the stranger turned his eyes and, for the first time, met Michael's. With an absolute pleading in his voice, he continued:

"...don't look behind you."

And with that, the stranger turned on his heels and slowly walked away. Michael waited there for several minutes, unsure of what to do. Then, feeling silly, he turned and went home.

He arrived feeling ill-at-ease from his dealings with the stranger. The man was mad–that much was obvious–but Michael couldn't help but wonder at him.

What kind of world would it be, he thought, *to believe all of that, and to know with absolute certainty that it was all real. To see what watched from behind people, and what lived under the bed.*

He got undressed and walked across the room to his bed, but stopped in mid-step. He turned to the mirror which sat above his dresser and stared at it, looking for what he knew couldn't possibly be there. He watched for several minutes while his heart pounded and every hair on his body stood on end. He had thought that, just for an instant, something had been watching him. Something that wanted to look like him, like his reflection, but had no humanity in its eyes or movements. And its teeth... oh, its teeth...

He shook his head to dislodge the sudden urge he felt to run, then he took a deep breath and crawled between the sheets.

And as the minutes turned to hours and he lay there still, unmoving but awake, he heard the faintest scratching coming from underneath his bed. *Rats,* he thought, as the scratching turned to a soft, rhythmic breathing. *Very big rats.*

Even as he justified it to himself, and as a great-many limbs curled around him in an embrace, he remembered the look in the crazed stranger's eyes, and the advice he had given him:

"*Don't look.*"

93

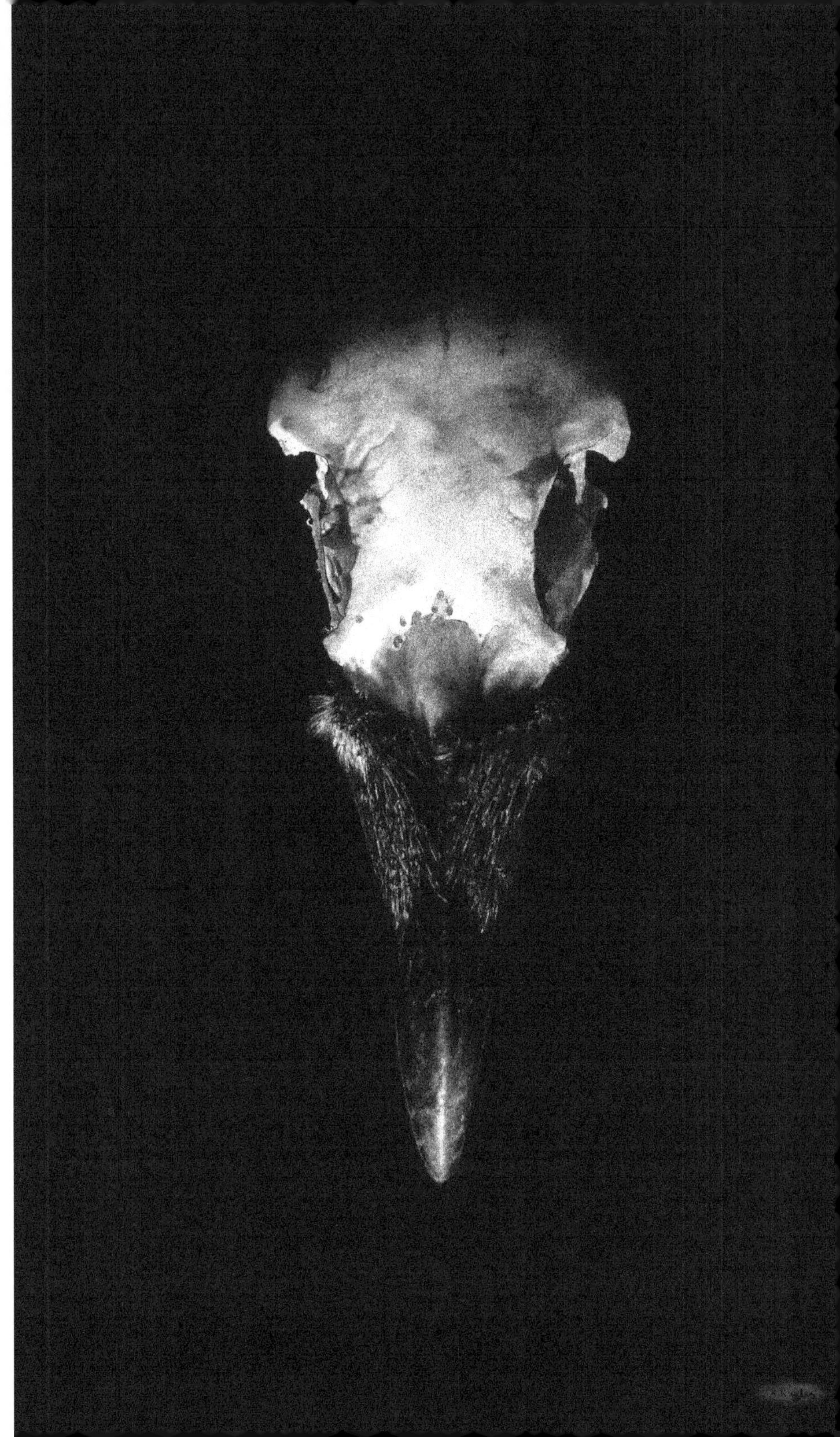

Finders Keepers

Ash poked her head out of the door and into the morning sun. Sure enough, her hungry friends sat in their usual spot atop a dead elm tree, waiting patiently for her to emerge.

One of them signaled to the others, and a small murder of crows landed in the yard in front of her. She smiled at them.

"Good morning," she said, cheerfully.

The one she thought of as Brutus cawed at her in reply. He was always the most vocal and the largest of the group, and demanded first taste of anything she gave them.

Ash knelt down and opened her hands. Brutus glanced at her empty palms, but didn't stir. He tilted his head at her, and she smiled wider.

"Very good," she said. She reached into her pocket and pulled out several un-shelled peanuts. She piled six in one hand and four in the other, then closed her fists and made a few complicated movements in the air while the murder watched, then she put her hands behind her back. "Okay," she said. "Choose."

Brutus hopped forward and began pacing back and forth in front of Ash's knees. Finally, he stopped and gently nipped at her left knee. Ash laughed, delighted, and opened her left hand to reveal six peanuts.

Brutus eyed the peanuts, then looked at her. He cawed when she refused to set them on the ground.

"It's okay, Brutus. I won't hurt you," she whispered.

Brutus stared at her for a long moment, seeming to weigh his options. He walked over to her palm, still staring Ash in the eye, then he quickly turned, grabbed a peanut, and hopped away.

Ash laughed and placed the rest of the peanuts on the ground, including several more from her pockets. Brutus, who had finished shelling and sampling his own, made a slight guttural noise to the rest of the murder, who happily fell upon the pile of nuts.

Ash stood up and left them to their feast. She locked up her home and went into town. She went into a small grocery store, grabbed a hand-basket, and started doing her shopping. "Can I help you find anything, miss?" a redheaded clerk asked as she paced up and down the aisles.

"No, thanks," Ash replied. *I'll need eggs, heavy cream, vanilla,* she thought, going through her mental checklist. *Nutmeg, butter, cinnamon, some twinkling fairy lights...*

She paused in the aisle, wondering where that last thought had come from. She shook her head and turned around, colliding with a man who was standing behind her. "Oh! I'm so sorry," she said.

The man, dressed in shades of black, made no reply. He only stared at her, expressionless.

"I uh... I didn't see you there," Ash continued.

The man tilted his head at her, his eyes jotting to her basket then back to her face. Ash slowly backed away from the man and carried on with her shopping. Every so often she would stop and look around, only to see the same strange man peering around a corner at her.

When she was finished, she went to the register and asked the clerk "Do you have any idea who that man is?"

"Which?" the clerk replied, looking around the room.

Ash turned to point him out. He was standing, awkwardly, behind a stand selling various sauces. "That one," she said.

The clerk shrugged. "Never seen him before," he said. "If he gives you any trouble, feel free to come back and I'll take care of it."

Ash rolled her eyes. "Right. Thanks." She packed her groceries into some bags and left. If the strange man followed her out, she never noticed him, so she returned home. She put her shopping down on the porch and looked for what was usually waiting for her.

She was not disappointed.

Neatly piled, exactly where she had left the peanuts, were several small items: an old coin, a bent screw, some tinsel, and a small, chopped-up strand of fairy lights. She smiled and looked to the top of the long-dead elm. Brutus stood in his usual spot, and Ash bowed to him. He cawed in response.

Ash collected her treasures and went inside. As she was unpacking her shopping, she was surprised to find that a large knife had found its way into her bags.

The next day, Ash poked her head out of her doorway to begin her morning feeding routine. She glanced up at the top of the elm tree, but Brutus wasn't there. Only four sets of black, beady eyes greeted her. "Brutus?" she called.

She heard him caw, and he hopped out of the bushes below the elm tree. "What are you doing down there?" she asked, walking toward him. When she got closer, she understood – Brutus's wing was mangled and bent, broken back at an awkward, painful angle.

Ash gasped and frowned. "You poor dear," she said, sitting down next to him. "What happened to you?"

Brutus cawed at her and pecked at the bulge in her pockets. Ash sighed. Instead of making him work for it, she placed a small handful of peanuts directly in front of Brutus and another pile nearby for the other birds. The rest ate happily, but Brutus ate slowly, constantly glancing over his shoulder and into the street that ran by her house.

An old, black sedan sat there, its engine running. Ash hadn't thought anything of it at first, but the longer it lingered, the stranger it seemed. She got up and walked toward the car. As she approached, laughter erupted from the dark window, and it sped off down the road.

Ash turned back to see Brutus standing next to her, silently staring at the retreating car. She smiled at him.

Before the day was through, she had built Brutus a small covered box filled with papers and bits of ribbon, and left him to frolic in it while she made dinner.

That night, while she was checking on Brutus, snug in his recovery nest, she spotted something where she had left the bird's food earlier in the day. She walked over, picked it up, and held it up to the light.

It was a tooth, root and all, and it had been capped in gold. She looked back to Brutus, who made a happy, quiet noise, and nested deeper into the papers.

The next morning started like any other day. Ash got up, got ready, and peered outside, but today, there were no tiny eyes watching her, waiting for their breakfast. She searched the recovery box for Brutus, but he, too, was gone.

Ash stifled a sob, wondering where her friends could be. They'd never missed a meal before, even going so far as to peck at her window if she slept-in too late.

She checked the tops of trees all around, but there wasn't a crow in sight. *Grapes,* she thought suddenly, remembering how much the murder loved them. She ran to the store in town, thinking that she might bribe them to return.

Going inside, she approached the same redheaded clerk who was working the other day. "Excuse me," she started. "Do you have any fresh grapes?"

The clerk turned, his cheek swollen and bruised. He thought for a moment, then snapped his fingers. "I think we just got some in today," he said, locking out his register. "Follow me. You can have your pick of the bunch."

Ash followed him to the back of the store and through a set of double doors leading to their loading dock and storage area.

"Am I allowed to be back here?" she asked, startled at the dirty surroundings compared to the pristine and bright storefront.

"Sure, so long as I'm with you," the clerk replied, and smiled. "Right over here. They just came in."

He lead her to an even darker area in the far corner of the building and Ash looked around. "I don't see anything."

"No, I guess you wouldn't," the clerk said, suddenly giggling to himself. "We don't get grapes in until next month."

"What the hell?!" Ash shouted. "Why would you waste my time like this?"

He stared at her, his eyes wide. "Did... did you like the knife?" he asked.

"What?"

The clerk burst into laughter. "Poor girl, all alone," the clerk said in a teasing tone, pulling a pistol from his pocket.

Ash looked around the area for something to beat him senseless with, but there was nothing nearby. She was planning how best to attack with her bare hands when someone tackled the clerk from behind.

The strange, black-clad man she had been followed by the other day stood up and kicked at the clerk on the ground with his heavy boots. The clerk scurried away and stood up. "You again?" he shouted. "Didn't you learn from the last time, you freak?!"

It was then that Ash noticed the strange man's mangled arm, twisted and broken, hanging at his side. The strange man glanced at Ash, then over to the gun, then back to her.

Ash nodded. Together, they charged the clerk.

The clerk raised his pistol.

And fired.

The next day, Ash was lying in bed, still awake from the night before, starring at the ceiling. She had beaten the clerk's head into the concrete until he was senseless – perhaps dead. She hadn't asked when the police had finally told her that she could go home.

She did wonder what had happened to the strange man who had helped her. He had been shot, she was sure of that, but the police said that nobody had checked into any hospitals or morgues with a gunshot wound. Maybe he was scared, she thought. But what of, she couldn't imagine.

A tapping at her window startled her. She looked up and saw

one of her crows sitting on her windowsill, eyeing her sideways. Ash smiled, and nodded to the crow.

She went outside with her usual pocketful of treats. The rest of the murder was present, but not Brutus. She sighed, heavily, fearing the worst, but left the food for the others and watched them as they happily devoured it.

A few hours later, she looked back at the spot she'd left the food. There, she found a small string, a shiny pebble, a bullet casing, and the skull of a crow, cleaned and bleaching in the sun.

A Question of Evil

The wind was cold, making the night a cruel, unforgiving one. The few people who wandered the street were in search only for their own poisons and were unaware, unfeeling, or uncaring of the weather.

Apep approved entirely. Nights like this reminded him of the old country, in another time, when nights were his to command. It stirred a mischievous mood in him as he walked down the street. At a crosswalk he paused, looked around for any onlookers, then unzipped his trousers and started to piss.

A black liquid streamed out of him, spreading along the pavement. Soon, it covered the entire crosswalk. He zipped up his trousers, knelt down, pursed his lips, and blew on the steaming puddle. In seconds, the crosswalk was a solid sheet of ice. He smiled at his handiwork, then went back into the shadow of a shop doorway to await his victim.

A few minutes later, a young woman ambled out of a nearby pub. She strolled an awkward path along the sidewalk toward Apep and the frozen crosswalk. A little way down the street, a car started. Apep watched the driver attempt to wipe off the dew-dusted, foggy windshield, and smiled. He whispered words of urgency. Carried on the wind, his voice reached the driver's ear, who stopped trying to clear her windshield and pulled into the street.

The drunken woman reached the crosswalk, paused, then put her foot out.

"Carol!" shouted someone from behind her. She stepped back just as the car hit the ice. The car slipped, turned, and slammed into another car parked across the street. Apep was appalled. He walked over to the pile of twisted metal and broken glass that was once two vehicles and was not surprised to see the driver was unhurt.

He turned and walked toward the pub, growling under his breath. He could see the driver's future. She would leave a note on the car she hit. The owner and her would meet to discuss the damages, go on to date, fall in love, and eventually adopt a child together barring any god's further involvement. He took some solace from the life of the drunken woman who was nearly hit, who would go on to defraud several thousand people of their life savings, but it wasn't nearly as fun as what he had planned.

He tried to gauge if the events that passed had made the world better or worse, all told, and was frustrated to find that he couldn't tell.

He walked into the pub and spotted a familiar face sitting at the bar. The man, his radiant face beaming, smiled at him. "Hello, old snake," he said, raising his glass in greeting.

"Don't you 'hello' me. Did you see that nonsense? Ridiculous!" Apep grumbled, sitting next to the other man. "Why did you call out to the girl? You've no right to interfere with my affairs!"

The man's smile didn't even flicker. It simply went from one of pleasant greeting to the cold, stark warning of a predator showing its teeth. "First off, I have every right and you know it. Second, I didn't call to her. Someone else must have." He sipped his drink.

Apep swore under his breath. "If I thought you were capable of lying, I'd have your throat out of you in an instant!"

"I'm sure you'd try, but I can't. Besides, you'd miss me." He finished his drink and raised his hand to the bartender. "Another for me, and for my friend... how does a pint of old peculiar sound?"

Apep rolled his eyes. "Fine, damn you," he relented.

"Not hardly," the other man balked. "So, what brings you to me tonight?"

Apep stared at the bar, wishing his drink was already there, not daring to meet the other man's eyes. "Beelzebub is dead," he said, finally.

The other man furrowed his brow. "What?"

"He's dead. I watched it happen."

"How?"

Apep shrugged. "The usual way. Not enough servants left to sustain him. No true believers of him as he was. Nothing left. Nothing at all."

They both sat in silence for several moments as their drinks arrived. Apep finished his in one continuous swallow, then ordered another.

"Old Beelz... You know, at one time, everyone thought that he'd be around forever." The other man shook his head, sadly.

"Yeah, but everyone thought the same about Ra, and Odin, and Apollo..."

"I thought you killed Ra," the man accused, though not impolitely.

"I did, every night, for sodding centuries. But the bastard would always come back in the morning. And then, one morning, he didn't wake up." Apep took a drink of his beer. "You know, sometimes I actually miss the pompous idiot?"

The other man smiled, but hid it behind his glass. "So, how many does that leave on your end of things?"

"Well, there's Set, and –"

The man shook his head. "Set is gone. Years ago, now."

"What? How?"

"Horus and him had a fight. They both lost." The man shrugged.

Apep nodded. "What about Anubis?"

"Who can tell?"

They both laughed, but not in joy. It was the laughter of funerals and battlefields – a melancholy, half-mad grasp at happiness. They both finished their drinks. More arrived, un-ordered but welcome.

The other man brightened. "What about Nox?"

Apep shook his head. "She's alive, but she's... different. She's grown cold and crazy ever since the mortals started leaving the planet and shooting holes in her. I think it's only a matter of time before..."

The man nodded. "So... that leaves..."

"Just me, I think," Apep said, coldly, then he turned to the other man and smiled. "Looks like you just might outlast me, afterall."

The man sipped his drink, then shook his head and pushed it to the far side of the bar. He turned to the bartender. "Bring me your best scotch," he said.

"You *will* outlast me, won't you?" Apep pried.

The man shrugged. "I honestly don't know. I haven't seen any of the others in a long, long time." He sipped at his scotch, then swirled it in the glass. "I've been feeling a bit tired as of late."

Apep stared at his companion, his jaw hanging low. "But... that's not right. There are millions of mortals who pray to you. How can –"

The man shook his head. "They pray to a thought of me, a symbol of me, but to *me*? The real me? Only a few. Far, far too few, I'm afraid."

"But that doesn't make any sense. They still believe in the other one. Surely you'd get some sort of runoff from that?"

The man laughed. "Oh, Him. He's been gone for quite some time, too. Maybe not dead, but dormant. No," he breathed, "my time is limited."

They drank together in silence for a while, neither of them wanting to ask, but both wanting to know. Finally, Apep cleared his throat. "How did this happen?" he asked.

The other man raised his eyebrows and let out a deep breath, slowly. "Times change. The Unnamed hold sway, now. The ambiguous gods."

Apep hissed. "Those bastards annoy the hell out of me. They can't even pick a damn goal."

"You think they're agents of chaos?"

"Not at all. Chaos is a goal, and one I would quite enjoy. But they can't even get that far. Sometimes their actions bring more order than chaos, more evil than good the next. I mean, look at that damn invention of theirs! Kills millions of the mortals in an instant, thousands more from cancer later on, and then they go and provide electricity and medical treatments with it! I just wish they'd make up their minds."

Apep finished his beer. Another arrived.

The other man didn't move. He simply smiled at his drink. "It won't be long now, I think."

"What?"

"I've got very little time left." He took a drink of his scotch and sighed. "I had hoped to be able to get more done, you know? But after everything..." He shook his head, sadly. "I really am tired. Maybe it would be nice to rest."

Apep stared at his companion, not understanding. "But you've been here since the beginning. You helped create some of these mortals! You stood up for them when He was being cruel and unfair! How can they not remember you?"

The man only smiled.

Apep took a pull off his pint, then sat in silence for several moments. "Any regrets?" he asked, finally.

His companion turned to him, exuding joy and nostalgia. "One or two, perhaps. But the big stuff? Never."

Apep nodded, then chuckled under his breath. "Bastard," he said, not unkindly. "Here's to you." He raised his half-full pint of beer, and his companion raised the remnants of his scotch.

"It was fun while it lasted," his companion added.

They drank.

A short while later, Apep walked out of the pub, confident that he would never see his friend again. He saw a statue depicting old Apollo standing in a proud pose, covered in pigeon droppings, and he wondered, briefly, if that was their ultimate fate as gods. The great reward: guardian of park benches and bird shit.

He glanced out into the street to the crosswalk, still covered in ice. He thought about spreading a little more mischief, a little more evil, before the light drove him indoors, but, somehow, his heart just wasn't in it anymore.

He sighed, turned up his collar to the wind, and went home.

109

<u>Mercurial</u>

The mountain was colossal. The kind of mountain a child might draw – all peak at too-sharp of an angle. And yet, on they went, up a road that made no physical sense in the world. They didn't drive for the very logical reason that the hill was simply too steep for cars, but nobody complained, nobody asked why the road existed in the first place, nobody was even tired as they neared a building at the top.

Rene knew it was a dream, then. In reality, all of his travel companions, himself included, would have fallen over from exhaustion before now. He looked at them, one at a time, letting the dream continue unharmed.

There were friends he didn't see any longer in the waking world, people who had grown out of touch as the years went by, as children, relationships, and jobs took over their lives. There was also two people Rene never thought he would see or speak to ever again: Kristof, who died in a tragic accident, and Thana, who took her own life.

Rene smiled. Thana winked at him with her green eyes, just as she'd done so many times in life, and his heart ached at the memory.

And then he saw someone he didn't recognize. A young woman walked in the middle of the group, but she moved awkwardly, as if her limbs had too many joints or if she didn't have enough of them. Rene moved closer to her as they walked up the mountain. "Hello," he said, and she turned to him, her eyes oddly wide. "I'm afraid I've forgotten your name."

"Oh... Um... " Her eyes stayed fixed on Rene's. "Gertrude," she admitted, finally.

"Really? Well, hello Gertrude. I'm sorry, I don't think I recognize you."

"You wouldn't," she said, smiling with just her teeth. "I'm new."

Rene walked next to her until they reached the summit and the small building there. They stood in a parking lot overlooking a valley thousands of feet below. Rene glanced over the sheer cliff and whistled. Then he looked back to the group. Gertrude still hadn't blinked. Rene found himself staring at her while the others mingled, blinking his own eyes repeatedly as if to make up for it.

Gertrude finally noticed what he was doing, looked around to see that no one else was watching, and blinked, but not with her eyes. Instead, she blinked with her whole face – her eyebrows pushing her eyelids closed, her nose wrinkling with the effort.

Rene shook his head and went to talk to Kristof and Thana. "She's a weird one," he said, tilting his head toward where he'd left Gertrude.

"Who is?" Kristof asked.

Rene turned to point her out, but she was gone. Instead, there was a small, stone bench sitting conspicuously where she'd been standing. "...Nevermind," Rene said, turning back to his friends.

The dream was wonderful. Rene spent time with each of his forgotten friends, laughing at old jokes, introducing new ones, but he spent the majority of his time with Thana. They had always had a bit of a connection when she was alive, and Rene had missed having her in his life.

Hours went by, and the gathering of friends was winding down. Rene was saying his goodbyes, but nobody had seen Kristof in quite some time. "I'll go find him," Thana volunteered. Rene knew something was wrong, that he shouldn't let her go by herself, but, in the way of dreams, he couldn't say anything to stop her.

When some time had gone by, Rene finally went looking for his friends. His search took him out to the parking lot with its beautiful views. Gertrude stood at the guard rail, staring at the sunset. She spoke without turning around. "You're waking up soon, aren't you?" she asked.

Rene paused in his stride a few feet behind her. "What? How did you-"

"Answer me!" she demanded.

"...I think so. It feels like it, anyway."

Gertrude lowered her head. "I see," she said.

"Have you seen Kristof and Thana? They've gone missing."

Gertrude nodded, still not turning toward him.

"Where were they?" Rene asked.

She shrugged. "I don't see how it matters. They weren't the dreamer. They weren't important."

"Gertrude, where are they?"

She turned to Rene. "They aren't here anymore." She walked

over and took him by the hands. "Please help me," she begged. "Don't wake up! I don't want to die."

Her eyes had somehow changed. They were green, now, when they had been brown. Rene pulled himself loose from her grasp. "Where did they go?!"

Gertrude sighed. "They wouldn't help me convince you to stay, don't you understand?" She walked over to the guardrail. Quietly, she whispered "They didn't even scream on the way down."

Rene ran to the railing and looked over the sheer cliff. Far below, he could just make out two familiar shapes. He stood there, speechless, his eyes filling with tears.

"Maybe that's the answer," Gertrude said from next to him. "Maybe I can beat you out of the dream."

Rene looked over at her just in time to see her smile, awkwardly, and then she winked, and threw herself over the edge. He watched her fall, watched her shift and change shape as she fell through the air. Suddenly that wink and her strange looking eyes made a kind of sense. They looked so odd because they weren't hers, at all.

Rene awoke covered in sweat, gasping for air. He sat up and took several deep, unsteady breaths, coming to grips with reality.

That's when he saw Gertrude.

She was standing at the front of his bed, moving her hands through the air, slowly, simply experiencing reality. Rene tried to scream, but nothing came out.

Gertrude turned to him and placed one too-long finger on her lips. "Shhh..." she hissed.

She backed away, growing larger with each step, smiling her awkward smile or, possibly, showing-off the fangs that grew there. Slowly, she merged into the wall, morphing into it until Rene couldn't tell where she ended and the wall began.

Finally, he screamed.

Rene left his apartment that night, arriving at a friend's house half-dressed and half-mad. Two days later, he returned. The front door was wide open. His room had been ransacked, but nothing was missing. His friends tried to convince him that it was just a nightmare, that he had left his door open in his panic and someone had gotten in and trashed the place, and sometimes Rene believed them.

But sometimes, he'll be walking down a crowded street, and someone unknown to him, someone new, will be walking by like they don't have enough limbs, or perhaps have too many, and they'll look at him with recognition, and they'll wink at him with familiar eyes, and he knows that she's out there, that she is improving her performance, and that it's only a matter of time before she comes to see him again.

<u>Cages</u>

Rain battered the rotting and degraded wooden shutters hanging on their long-rusted hinges. Wind bellowed through the holes in both the roof and the wall of the old asylum, greeting the decay of time like an old friend.

Stephen was pleased. He loved the rain, the slow patterns it pelted out on the roof, the beat of droplets as it leaked through ceiling, the feel of moisture in the air. He bristled at the sensation, sending a light mist against the wall. It hadn't been a pleasant day for Stephen, and the rain helped to relax him.

The bed frame creaked as he rearranged himself on the musty but wonderfully dry mattress, picking up an apple from under the bed and devouring it in one, massive bite. He took a deep, dusty breath and let it out into the fabric, staring out the open door of his bedroom, across the hall and out of the barred windows. The moon, peaking through the clouds, was a pale glow in his vision, but he stared at it just the same. A nearly constant companion, he greeted it whenever he could. It was his only regular visitor, and it was quiet and kept its distance, and he liked it for that.

Stephen laid in bed, listening to the little movements the rain always brought: the swelling of old wood, the scurrying of small creatures in the garden, the *scrape, scrape* of an overgrown tree limb upon a window.

Footsteps echoed down the hallway, drawing Stephen's attention – wet, hurried steps, and the alien friction of a rubber overcoat. Stephen quickly crawled under his bed and waited, his legs un-wittingly poking out from the back of the mattress. A man walked by Stephen's room, mumbling under his breath, his overcoat streaming small droplets of water onto the dirty floor. Stephen waited a moment for the man to pass, and then followed using paths that only he knew.

The man walked all the way to the old administrator's office. He walked in, removed his overcoat, hung it on a coat rack, and sat down behind a large oak desk, shuffling papers around and sighing. Stephen watched from a hole through the wall in the next room, hidden, curious.

The man at the desk opened the top drawer, mumbled something to himself, opened another. He pulled out a grey folder, opened it, and began checking boxes and writing in the blank spaces.

Stephen watched, fascinated. He particularly liked the scrape of pen on cheap paper, but not the strange, wet movement of the man's lips as he mouthed what he wrote. He could just make it out over the rainfall. "Patient exhibits severe delusions of grandeur, believing himself to be King George. Not the current George, but King George the First. Keeps threatening to invade other patients rooms. Demands taxes."

Stephen waited patiently while the man wrote, enjoying being hidden. When the man finished, he stood and went to a bank of filing cabinets against the far wall. He opened a drawer that had no bottom, thumbed through files that weren't there, then dropped his own file through the drawer and onto the floor. Not seeming to notice, he closed the drawer and went back to his desk.

Stephen looked on in fascination as the man gathered his overcoat and marched back down the hallway, his hobnailed shoes tapping on the stone floor. He listened to the man leave, only losing him as he passed into the main foyer. Stephen waited for an hour, nonetheless, before he moved, just in case he was wrong.

Satisfied, he went back to his room, dragging his fingers along the walls in time-worn grooves as he moved. The cool night air brought with it the dew. It glistened on the cold stone and shone like a million stars, reflecting the moonlight. Stephen watched the light dance as he passed and smiled in his own way.

The intruders weren't uncommon – strangely dressed figures going about their business, acting in a way that even Stephen felt was somehow very odd. He never approached them. He didn't like people, and given the very rare occasions that anyone saw him, it seemed people didn't like him, either.

He hated when they screamed.

And they always screamed when they saw him.

He entered his bedchamber and skittered his way to the far corner. Underneath some fallen plaster, tucked into the wall, he found his suitcase of treasures. He opened it, running his fingers along each unique piece therein. He took pleasure in the shapes and textures – the shine from a broken pair of glasses, the cold detail in a stone mini-figure, the almost liquid-smooth texture of an old, blue, glass marble, he delighted in them all.

"Cheater!" came the shout from the foyer down the hall. Stephen expertly placed his treasures all back into their places in his suitcase, closed the lid with one hand, and with two others, in one fluid motion, hid the suitcase in the wall once again.

"I didn't cheat! It went out, fair and square!" called another voice, higher than the first with a squeaky quality that set Stephen's brain on edge.

Stephen seemed to melt into the fabric of the shadows as he slowly made his way to the foyer.

Two children were gathered around a small chalk circle, arguing in the method of children everywhere: whoever has the last word, wins.

"It never left the circle! At best it stopped at the line, and that doesn't count!" the first boy shouted, gloating in his mastery of the rules.

"Most of it was out! It counts!" the screechy one replied. Stephen palmed his way closer to them, taking care to avoid the piles of debris on the ground, hiding his massive bulk in the shadow of a support column.

"Fine, then let's have a do-over."

"Fine! But I still say it was mostly out."

The boys carefully placed several glass spheres of differing size and color back into their appropriate locations from a moment ago, moving about in the gloom and moonlight with unsettling ease. Finally ready, the second boy took up position outside of the circle, and with a larger sphere resting against his thumb, his thumb building pressure against his pointer-finger, he shot the sphere into the circle.

Colored orbs flew every direction, rolling across the room, bonking off the stairs and columns, and one, a piercing blue glass marble, rolled right to Stephen. He picked it up without thinking, marveling at the color in the moonlight and the cold, smooth surface. He was so enraptured that he scarcely noticed the boy standing in front of him.

"Oh, hey mister," the boy said, holding his leather bag of winnings in his fist.

Stephen froze. This wasn't screaming. This was new.

"If you want to play, you've got to get your own marbles," the boy continued, reaching to take the treasure from Stephen's hand.

Stephen recoiled and backed up a pace, cradling the marble to his chest.

The boy gave him an appraising look, shrugged, and said "Fine, keep it, but I'm telling." And then he turned and calmly went back to his friend.

Stephen wasted no time. He retreated back to his room like a shadow from a torch, cradling his marble in a clenched fist all the while. He quickly crawled under the bed and listened for the children, but all was silent in the asylum.

Time began to turn the darkness into the pale grey of dawn, and Stephen emerged from the bed. He opened his hand to view his new prize and let out a dry gasp – the marble was gone. Frantic, he went to his suitcase, opened it, and saw the pale blue marble sitting there, undisturbed, just as he had left it.

He stared at it for a moment, confused but pleased, before he put the suitcase away again. A crash came from the floor above, and Stephen jumped in alarm. He crept through a hole in the ceiling and made his way to the noise.

"Don't!" someone cried. It was coming from the old washroom on the other side of the building. There was only one way into that room, the other side was locked with a massive iron gate, but there was a hole in the wall there, and if Stephen stood tall, he could just see through into the washroom.

Stephen peered through the hole, looking into the gloomy washroom. There was a child there, sitting with his back against the wall. He seemed to be bleeding, but Stephen wasn't sure of anything at the moment. A man walked into view holding an iron pipe.

"What did you tell them?" he said, and slammed the pipe into the wall next to the child's head. The child flinched and covered his head.

"I didn't tell them anything! I swear I didn't!" the child screamed.

Stephen was tired, and he was confused by the day he'd had, but he could tell the child didn't want to be there. He wanted to help, but he didn't know how. He moved his many hands to get a better grip on the wall, and a brick fell from his viewing hole. It crashed and shattered on the tile floor.

The man turned around, looking through the locked iron gate. "What the hell is that?!" he shouted. Stephen turned to where the man was facing, but he didn't see anything strange. Just his own shadow on the wall, cast by the morning light.

The man dropped the pipe and ran. Stephen listened to him as he went down the stairs, through the foyer, and out the front door.

The child stood up and looked through the bars at Stephen's shadow, a confused look on his face. He grasped at his wound, closed his eyes, and slowly shook his head. When he opened them again, the shadow was gone. He tilted his head to the side, looked around the room, then said to the open air "Thank you."

Stephen watched, hidden, as the child made his way out of the manor. Once he was safely away, Stephen went back up to his bed-room. There was a man sitting on the edge of his bed. He quickly hunkered down, flattening himself against the floor, emitting a noise that may have been a dry and brittle hiss, and shuffled into the corner.

"Who's there?" the man said, reaching into the darkness near the bed and producing a thin pair of glasses. He put them on and blinked at Stephen. "Oh, hello there. I didn't see you come in."

Stephen glanced one way and then the next, considering his retreat from this strange man without a scent.

"Is it time already?" the man asked, his thin hospital grey clothes blending him into the bed. He seemed to hear something from the doorway. "Oh, no, I'm just talking to my new friend, here." he replied to the door. "Only... he doesn't really say much." He turned to Stephen once again. "Are you mute? I'm the gardener here." He reached a hand out toward Stephen.

Stephen backed himself further into the corner, his hands pressing him up the wall. The man looked disappointed.

"That's alright," he said, nodding to the empty doorway. "They won't shake my hand, either." He looked almost familiar to Stephen, like a memory being viewed through the chaos of a kaleidoscope. The man stood up and pushed his feet into a pair of small, grey slippers. "I'll be along in a moment," he said to the air as he buttoned his shirt. After a few seconds, he turned and winked to Stephen, who considered retreating into the crypt and lamented not being able to reach the comfort and safety of his bed.

The man finished buttoning his shirt, then smiled. "Do you like apples?" he asked. Stephen bristled. The man walked toward Stephen, still smiling, and reached out his hand. Stephen looked from the smiling face to the outstretched hand and back again, darting glances toward the door and the hole in the ceiling, but the strange man didn't flinch. He didn't retreat, nor did he reach further. He simply waited, pleasantly.

Stephen focused on the hand, watching for any movement, and slowly, as if sneaking up on a nightmare, he reached a hand forward. Inch by inch, he moved closer, closer, closer until he was almost touching the strange man's hand. He locked his gaze onto the man's blue/grey eyes, then grasped at the proffered hand...

...and passed right through it as if it were fog. Confused, Stephen tried to grip it again, and again he passed through. He looked up at the man, who only chuckled. "Well, that's a thing," he said, and chuckled once again. And then, slowly, he faded away.

Stephen blinked his many eyes at the darkness, then crawled into his bed and sulked. There were too many visitors for one day, too many odd humans doing odd things. Outside, the rain was just beginning to fade away, and he had wanted to go explore the garden today for any fresh apples, but no. Today had been too strange, already. He settled down onto the mattress, and tried to relax. Soon, he was sound asleep.

125

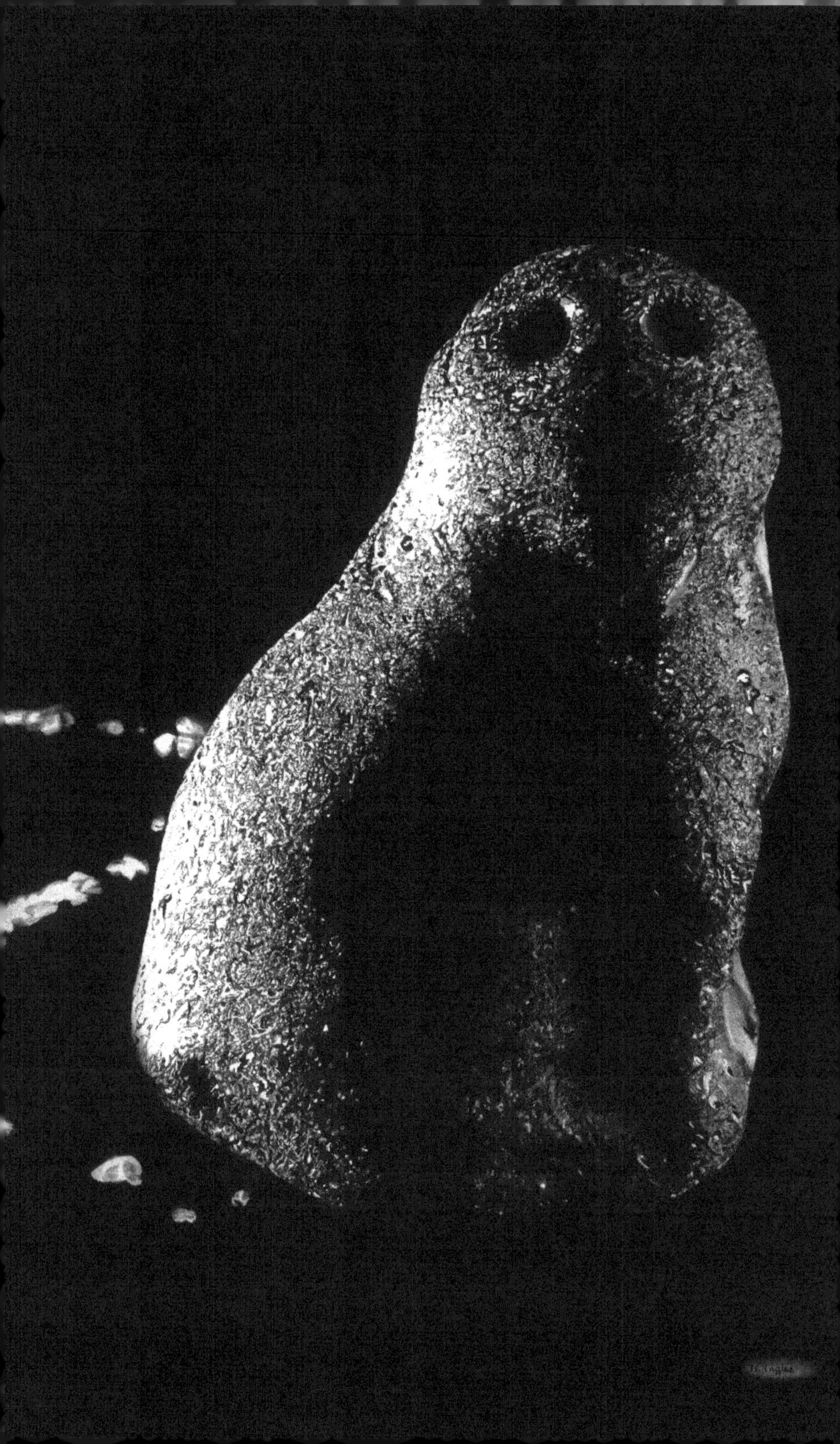

<u>Charmed</u>

The sun was low in the hills, hanging in clouds of orange and pink and a blood red sky. Their bags still lay scattered on the living room floor, being unpacked one piece at a time as they required things from the trip.

Neither of them had gone back to work after returning from their vacation. They had called-in every outstanding sick day, every floating holiday that they had to prevent losing their jobs, but they'd given up on returning the phone calls and the urgent texts. There just didn't seem to be much point to it all anymore. Claire and Anthony spooned on the sofa, watching an unfortunate infomercial on a "new and improved" way to cook fish. Neither of them knew where the remote was.

"People have been eating fish for millions of years," Claire said. "You'd think we'd know how by now."

Anthony didn't reply. He simply lay there, unblinking, stroking

Claire's hair, remembering the trip they had taken.

"Do you want to get something delivered soon?" Claire asked, elbowing him in the side. Anthony grunted a semi-positive tone. "Anthony?" Claire rolled over and burrowed her head into his chest. "Do you still hear the voices?"

Their vacation was a long time coming. They were both professionals. They wore suits and worked in offices where how well you bantered with your coworkers was just as important as your ability to do your job, and they both wanted to go someplace where they didn't speak the language, but where they could be pampered.

They settled, after very little research, on an area of Egypt far away from the more well-known ruins, but that still had highly recommended hotels and restaurants. They were deeply disappointed that most of the staff, the cabbies, the servers and hosts, and several people who were vending items in the street markets all spoke English.

"At least we won't have trouble in an emergency?" Anthony said. Claire rolled her eyes.

They had been on vacation for three days. The shops and restaurants nearby to their hotel had lost their allure, and they had spent the day exploring further areas on foot, trying to find something interesting to take home with them.

Claire had found a vendor of spices and dried fruits and was neck-deep in negotiation with an irritated shop owner over the price, so Anthony took his leave of her and went across the street to a seller of oddities and souvenirs. He looked over the compressed sand sculptures of the pyramids, the plastic recreations of reed ships and bobble-head figures of palm trees with sunglasses, groaning internally. He nodded politely at the vendor. "Sorry to be a pest," he started, "but I don't suppose you have anything a little... different for sale?"

The vendor stared at him for a moment, then smiled. "Sir would like something *special* to take home with him?" he asked, winking as obviously as he could.

"Oh? Oh! Uh, no. Nothing like that," Anthony flustered, holding up his hands in innocence. "I'm just looking for something a little bit more unique than these."

The vendor nodded in understanding. "I have a few things you might like," he said, and pulled out a small tray of items from below the counter.

Anthony looked over the pieces in the tray, the vendor describing them as he went. There were bracelets made by local craftspeople using local materials, some rings and pendants of silver and gold, and then there was a collection of things which were very obviously not local. "What are those?" Anthony asked.

"Ah. Well, you see, Egypt is very old. We were trading throughout the Mediterranean and all along the coasts of Europe and Africa before Troy fell and spawned the refugees who formed Rome. And in all that time, we have collected things from other places," he explained, indicating the jade tiles and ancient coins from places Anthony had never heard of.

He spotted a small figure in the pile, scarcely an inch tall, made of a strange, dark stone that had, at some point, been tumbled and chipped among other stones or in the sea. "Where did this come from?" he asked.

The vendor examined the figure, running his fingers over the deeply carved lines making up the body of a cat in a sitting position, noting the oddly rounded face and deep holes left there. They gave Anthony the impression that it was watching the both of them in shocked interest.

"I don't know, sir," the vendor admitted. "It could be one of ours, but it could have just as easily come from anywhere else."

"You think so?"

The vendor smiled. "It's a cat, sir. People like cats."

Anthony laughed, and he bought the figure. The vendor put it in a small velvet bag, and Anthony put the bag in his pocket. He made it back to his wife just in time to see the end of the negotiations, which settled on a price just a little more than the shop owner had originally quoted.

They did, finally, move from the sofa, if only because it was more comfortable to spend the night in their bed. But neither of them slept. They lay there, motionless, barely even breathing, hands resting against one another for the reassurance touch brings.

They would be out of money in two weeks. Every drop of savings would be gone, every hiding spot for cash raided. Anthony tried to do the math in his head, and was surprised to find that he didn't care.

Yes, rent was coming due.

Yes, food was getting scarce.

But none of that mattered, anymore. Anthony wondered if, perhaps, it never did.

That night, Claire and Anthony ate dinner at a fantastic place about a mile from their hotel. The food was vegetarian, and it was absolutely delicious. Anthony reached into his pocket to pay for their meal and pulled out the little velvet bag along with his money.

"What's that?" Claire asked, reaching for the bag.

Anthony quickly snatched it away from her. "Nothing. Just

something I picked up earlier."

She glared at him in mock outrage. "Are you buying weird shit again?" she asked, raising an eyebrow. "Did you find a monkey's paw? A cursed lamp?" She reached for the bag again, and Anthony pulled it away, laughing. "You know, vie haf vays of making you talk," she said in a bad German accent.

"Torture?" he smiled.

"Of a sort." She smiled back.

They both erupted in laughter, drawing pleasant looks from the other diners. "It's just an old figure," Anthony admitted, dumping it out of the bag and into his hand. "Barely worth mentioning."

He stared at the figure in his hand for several seconds, looking into the hollow eyes, stroking the rough stone. Somewhere on the edge of hearing, something called his name...

Claire poked him in the side. "Anthony," she called, moving his face in front of hers. "Did you stroke-out there for a second?"

Anthony shook his head. "Sorry, I was miles away." He stood up and put the figure back in his pocket. "Do you want to head back to the hotel? he asked. "I'm kind of tired all of a sudden."

The rest of the evening passed pleasantly. They put a movie on their tablet and fell asleep in each other's arms.

It was still dark when Claire awoke alone in the hotel bed. She could hear something coming from across the room, a kind of halting, staggered whisper.

"Anthony?" she called, but the whisper kept on. She turned on the bedside lamp and saw Anthony, nude, squatted down in the corner, whispering into his fists that he held clasped together in front of him. She went to him and gently laid her hand on his shoulder.

He jerked back, beads of sweat flinging from his face. His eyes were wide, and wild, and mad. He pulled Claire down to the floor with him and hissed "Do you hear it?"

"What? I-"

"Do you hear it!?" Anthony shouted, then whispered "It won't be quiet. It keeps talking, telling me things, things I don't want to know. Things I shouldn't know..." He opened his fist and held out his hand to her. There, in his palm, lay the small cat-like figure she'd seen at dinner. "Listen," Anthony breathed, holding the figure up to Claire's ear.

She tried to push his hand away, but it was already too late. She no longer wanted to.

Claire opened her eyes. There was a stench in the air much more repulsive than her own unwashed body. She looked over at Anthony and saw what it was. She couldn't tell how long he'd been dead, but it was long enough for rot to set in.

She gathered together what strength she had left and sat up. *When was the last time I ate?* she thought. She couldn't remember. Her memories were cloudy, unorganized. Nothing seemed to make sense. She stood up, slowly, unsteadily, and shuffled down the hallway to the living room. She fell to her knees next to Anthony's luggage and felt a bone snap like a dry stick. She paid it no mind. After all, it didn't really matter.

She dug through his suitcase until she found a small, velvet bag. She pulled the tiny figure from the bag and held it to her ear. She closed her eyes and breathed deep.

And she listened.

133

The Borrower

It was a cloudy, moderately warm day. Perdita sat in her kitchen, staring out into her garden and the cemetery beyond, wishing it were colder. She looked at the confused plants – some wilting to brown, others budding and flowering, and knew that something was wrong. She sighed.

It had been an oppressively hot summer, and she had been looking forward to the day she would finally be able to explore the graves. It was one of the few places in the city where nature was allowed to grow unimpeded, and she'd missed the wildness of nature ever since she moved here.

Movement caught her eye. Through her window, she watched as a slender fox crawled through a hidden hole in her garden wall. It paused to bite at its backside a moment, then straightened, sat, and looked around. It froze when it spotted Perdita spying on it through the window. Slowly, it rose back to its feet and began to back away.

Then, all at once, it turned and dove back under the wall.

"That does it," Perdita said to the universe at large. She stood up, put on her boots, grabbed some grapes and seeds to snack on, then went outside and climbed over the garden wall.

She landed in soft earth, moss, and grass, and immediately she felt more at home. It was almost as if she were welcome, there. Graveyards had always been described to her as eerie, tragic places, but she found that they were calming, sombre, somewhat wild when left to their own devices.

And this one had been. Ivy grew up and around many of the headstones, blotting out the name of the dead below. She strolled through the underbrush, careful not to step on any of the burial plots lest she be dragged under by a vengeful corpse like the urban legends told. Besides, stepping on them felt like a rude thing to do.

She was moving further and further back into the older parts of the cemetery, looking for the oldest grave; looking for the guardian.

She didn't know when the practice began. She only knew what her grandmother had told her – that the first creature buried in the graveyard would be kept there, forever, as its guardian. Some believed that the guardian was there to help the dead move-on, to guide them to the other side, but Perdita's grandmother always thought that was rubbish.

"People will always believe a comfortable lie over a dangerous truth," she could say, while in her cups. If pressed, she would go on to say that nobody would have given a guide the title of guardian, but would say nothing more about it.

Perdita found an old, overgrown path that wove its way along the small hills in the yard, much more organic than the newer rows and columns that were organized against any creativity or beauty. She followed it past an old, dead tree, planted even before the markers and statues came in.

A flash of orange showed that she had found her friend the fox. It had poked its head up between the roots of the old tree, and as she watched, three smaller heads popped up to join it. She was being watched by eight curious eyes as she passed. She did her best not to disturb them. This was their home, and she was just a guest here.

She made her way along. The identical markers made way for more unique ones, unique markers fell away to roughly rounded stones and strangely ornate statuary, testament to the poor and rich peoples buried here.

A few yards further on, she stumbled into a small area full of long, wet grass. She laid out her jacket like a picnic blanket and sat down to eat her provisions. The drone and noise of the city seemed to be far away. She wondered, briefly, why the locals didn't come here more often.

She suddenly felt like she was being watched. She glanced around her, and spotted a blackbird sitting on the hand of a nearby statue, watching her eat with keen interest. Perdita smiled and tossed a few grapes on the ground below it, but the bird didn't move. She tried the seeds next, but still the bird held its place. She stood up and tossed more food, this time closer, and closer still. Finally, she tossed a grape directly at it, and it bounced off with a wet *plonk*.

Perdita laughed, finally realizing the bird she was trying to feed was part of the statue it rested on, and was made of stone. She smiled at her private embarrassment.

Finished with her snacks, she sat back and stared at the clouds, letting her mind wander. She thought of the dead buried here, if they might feel the pressure of the earth all around them, and if they wondered why they could no longer control their own rotten bodies. She shivered at the thought.

When the sun began to set, she gathered her jacket and started to make her way back to the garden wall. Her search for the guardian would have to wait for another day. She felt recharged and oddly happy, as if she had been needing this excursion for a long time.

Someone giggled. Perdita jumped and looked around, her eyes searching, but no one was there. Just the ornate statue she had seen before with the bird sitting on its-

The bird was gone, as were the grapes and seeds she had thrown.

Maybe I'm more exhausted than I thought, she wondered as she slowly backed away. The statue's eyes seemed to follow her, which, she knew, was the way of statues, and yet it unnerved her.

She made her way along the winding path, but couldn't shake the feeling that she was being watched. It wasn't the statues and it wasn't the patchwork of wildlife that lived in the cemetery. Something else, something older was watching her. Her grandmother's words came to her as if to fill the gap left by an unasked question.

"They wouldn't give a guide the title of guardian."

She paused. The long shadows mocked her vision as she darted her eyes all around. *How old is this place?* she thought, trying to recall. A gust of wind blew past, and it felt as if someone, something, had run its fingers through her hair.

Does the first thing buried in a graveyard have to be human?

She moved on, but the growing night made her path seem alien. She spotted the dead tree in the distance and headed toward it, looking over her shoulder every few steps, trying to catch sight of what she knew was stalking her.

Her skin tingled and her heart pounded. Every fiber of her being seemed to be screaming at her, warning of her of impending danger so ancient that it was felt instead of seen.

She looked back once again, tripped on a root of that long dead tree, and fell, hard, to the ground, striking her head on a gravestone, falling unconscious.

She awoke, and yet she didn't. She looked down at herself, lying in the dirt, and wondered if she were dead.

No, came the answer, echoing all around her through the graves and trees.

Perdita found that the shadows of the cemetery no longer kept their secrets from her. She witnessed hordes of the dead, translucent but human, wander around the paths and forgotten lanes around her, going about business of their own, and yet she was no longer afraid. Several of the dead stood and pointed. A few of them smiled at her. One smile child waved. She wondered if she were dreaming.

No, was the answer, seeming to be spoken by the air itself.

She closed her eyes. *What are you?* she thought.

There, so large that it appeared to be part of a distant hillside, blurred by the mist surrounding it, something turned toward her...

Perdita blinked in the harsh morning light. The dew hung heavily on her clothes and on the tree above her. There, nestled into the roots, sat a strange, black stone – a burial marker unlike anything she'd ever seen. She blinked again, and it was gone, blending back into the underbrush. She groaned. Her head felt as if it had been split in two.

She sat up and looked around, trying to recall tales the strange dream she'd had while she was unconscious, but her head seemed to throb worse the more she thought about it.

Slowly, unsteadily, she made her way back to the garden wall. Eight eyes watched her leave, and something else entirely merely observed her passing, keeping watch on the odd intruder.

In an Instant

He looked through his window and out onto the city.

It was raining. It was always raining. Living in Seattle, it seemed to do little else. He sighed. The rain was fitting, he thought. It should be raining on a night like this. He glanced down to the pistol in his hand, felt the weight of it along with the weight of his intention. He closed his eyes and took a deep breath.

A loud crunch came from behind him.

He turned to see a strange girl sitting on his sofa. She was loudly eating from a bag of popcorn. She took another great handful of fluffy kernels and attempted to shove them into her mouth, more missing than succeeding.

"How did you get in here?" he asked, putting the gun behind his back, reflexively.

"Aww... and it was just getting to the good part," the girl replied, setting the bag down and licking her fingers and palm, haphazardly. She looked over to the white wall next to the man. "It always makes such fun patterns on white. Maybe it's the contrast."

"What?"

She smiled. "The blood, silly. Well, and brains, of course. Oh! And tiny bits of skull." She squished her face into a look of mock disgust. "I always wonder if the brains know when they hit the wall. What do you think?" She turned to the man once again.

"Who are you? How did you get in here?" The man asked, tucking the gun into his belt behind his back.

"Awe, don't hide it. If you hide it, you'll never get to the good part." She tried to pout but her lip refused to cooperate. She attempted to glare at her own lip and tried again. Finally she succeeded, forcing her lower lip out on the third try and with some assistance from her hand. She pointed to the lip with pride and gave a thumbs-up to the man who stared in astonishment.

The man blinked at her. The girl stirred on his couch, uncomfortably looking to the floor and ceiling, avoiding his gaze. Finally, she cleared her throat, sat up straight, and raised her hand high, straining against gravity, staring at him in a perfect facsimile of seriousness. The man furrowed his brow at her, but shrugged and said "Yes?"

"Oh! Um... what was your question again?"

"Which one?"

She shrugged. "Which one do you want answered?"

"How did you get in here?"

The girl smiled. "That's a stupid question. Honestly. Given the choice, I would have asked for the meaning of life or how to get ten million dollars by tomorrow without getting arrested. No wonder you want to kill yourself." She rolled her eyes at him. "Anyway, I got in the same way I go anywhere."

"That's not funny," the man said, his voice cold.

"What's not?"

"You don't joke about suicide."

"Who's joking? That's not a prop gun in your belt, is it?" She leaned as far as she could while still sitting cross-legged on his couch and trying to peer behind his back. He turned to hide the pistol better. She fell to her side, legs still crossed, but now dangling in midair. "Totally real," she said, half muffled by the fabric of the cushion.

"That's not the point. You don't just make fun of things like that," he chided.

The girl righted herself. Her hair, tied horizontally on both sides of her head, flopped with the motion. "Wha? Who says? Seems like a silly rule to me."

"Just... people, okay? It's not something people do." The man let out an exasperated sigh.

The girl blinked at him. "That's a stupid rule. You're stupid. You should kill yourself." She smiled in triumph. When the man didn't say anything, she continued. "See? Because I made fun of it, and I'm people, kind of, more or less. So I win."

The man clenched and unclenched his jaw. "Get out," he said, simply.

"Don't wanna. You're fun." She picked a piece of fallen popcorn from her shirt and threw it at him. It bounced off of his face. "Besides, you need me."

"I need you?" he replied, incredulous. "I'm having the worst night of my life and you're making fun of it. Why the fuck would I need you?"

The girl stood up and smiled. "Because it isn't over yet," she said.

"What?"

"Your life. The bullet is still in the gun, so it isn't over yet. That's how cause and effect works. Well, usually. Most of the time, anyway."

He shook his head. "None of this makes sense," he said.

"It's suicide. Not making sense is par for the course." The girl strolled over to him, reached her arms out, and hugged him.

"What are you doing?" he asked, uncomfortably.

"I thought you might need a hug. Isn't that something people do? Wish they could have been there to hug them?"

"I don't know," he said, sadly.

"I'm also stealing this," she said quickly, pulling away and taking his pistol with her.

"Hey!" He reached out to grab her, but she spun out of his grasp. "Be careful with that! It's loaded!"

The girl rolled her eyes at him once again. "Well duh. Hard to kill yourself with an empty gun." She twirled the gun on her finger, expertly, then held the barrel to her nose and inhaled deeply. "I love that smell, don't you?"

"What smell?" he replied, annoyed.

"Gunpowder."

The rain pounded into the windows around them. In the distance, rolling in the bay, thunder echoed. "What? I haven't fired that gun in years."

The girl smiled at him mischievously. "Wanna bet?" She held the gun to her head, her smile frozen on her face, then she jerked her head to the side in mimicry.

He jumped.

She laughed and pointed at him. "Your face! You should see

your face!" She doubled over, clutching her stomach, still laughing. She glanced up again through her bangs, then laughed harder. "Seriously, do you have a mirror? It's so good."

"So... I'm..." he started.

"Shoosh!" She ran over to him and placed her finger on his lips. "Wait! Wait, you can almost...."

Thunder shook the windows in their frames sending them both to the ground covering their ears.

She rolled to her side, still holding her hands on her head, laughing. "There! See!"

"What the hell was that?!"

She rolled to her knees and poked him on the side of the head. The pain seemed to stay there, burning into his skull. "The gun, silly. It finally went off. You're on your way! Isn't this exciting?"

"The gun? But the gun is..." He looked around for the pistol. It had fallen to the floor during the thunder. "What are you talking about?" The pain in the side of his head grew. It felt as if a bug was biting him, tunneling into his skull.

"You'll figure it out," she said, still smiling. "In the meantime!" She jumped up and ran to the couch, where she plopped down and grabbed the bag of popcorn once again. She threw a handful in the general direction of her mouth, missing with every kernel but one. She munched down on it as the others landed all around her. "Let me know when you feel it coming out the other side," she said between chews. "I don't wanna miss *anything*."

"So, wait... I'm dying?"

"Sure. Unless you can survive a bullet to the brain." She furrowed her brow. "You wouldn't do that to me, would you? After all this effort?"

"Uh..."

She pulled her lower lip out once again and pointed at it, accusingly.

"I'll try not to," he finished.

"Eeeee!" the girl squealed. "Awesome. I love the splash. And the sound when the skull splits open. Unf! So good."

"You're crazy," he said.

The girl shook her head. "Which one of us just shot themselves, huh? Careful who you're calling crazy."

"That's different," he protested. "I had reasons to do what I did. You're just being cruel!"

"Am not."

"How are you not? You're making this worse at every turn."

"Nu-uh. You haven't even thought of why you did it since you pulled the trigger, have you? Not like you were before I showed up."

"Well yeah, but that's not-"

"Ta-dah!" She bowed from her sitting position on the sofa. "And you're welcome, by the way."

"So you're some kind of consolation prize? Keeping me company while I die?"

"Sure, if you like."

"But is that what you are?"

"No. Not even a little." She tilted the bag toward him. "Popcorn?"

The man stood there, the pain in his head progressing steadily.

"My brain itches," he said, finally. "How is that even possible?"

"It isn't. It can't. Your brain can't feel anything. You're just imagining it."

He pulled a chair out from the table and sat backwards in it, facing her, leaning on the back. "It doesn't feel like I'm imagining it."

She shrugged. "Good imagination?"

"Nah. I couldn't even imagine my way out of my problems." He sighed.

"I thought you said people shouldn't joke about suicide," she teased. He glared at her in response. "Oh come on. You've got a few minutes left at max, do you really want to spend it dwelling on why you killed yourself?"

He laughed through his nose and smiled. "I guess not."

The girl brought her knees up to her chin and rested her head on them. "So, what's it like? I mean, you said it itches, what else?"

"Actually, since you mentioned that it couldn't, it kind of went away."

The girl visibly deflated. "Well that's boring." She took a deep breath and let it out slowly. "I'm bored now."

"What, you want me to die quicker?"

She perked up. "Could you?"

"Shut up." He could feel pressure beginning to build on the other side of his head, near what would be the exit wound. He shivered at the thought. "Do you think anyone will miss me?" he asked, finally.

The girl stared at him. "You really are stupid, aren't you?" she replied. "I mean, I know, shot yourself, I should have known, but seriously..." She shook her head.

His face fell.

"Of course people will miss you," she finished.

He looked up again. "You think so?"

"Sure. For a little while, anyway. A couple years, maybe. A decade for people you were really close to. They'll all beat themselves up with how they wish they could have stopped you or how they should have seen it coming and all that. But eventually everyone will move on with their lives and forget about you. Everyone."

"What?"

"Well? What did you expect? People to pine over you and weep at your graveside for the rest of their lives?"

He shrugged. "I don't know. I guess I thought I was more important than that."

She giggled to herself. "Nope! But don't worry about it. Nobody is. People are built to cope and survive." She looked at the hole in the side of his head. "Uh... most people," she corrected herself.

The pressure in the side of his head turned into a burning ache. He closed his eyes to try to focus on something other than the pain.

"It's started out the other side, hasn't it?"

He nodded.

"Things will move quickly, now. It'll all be over soon." She reached out and put a hand on his shoulder. "Is there anything you wanna say before you go?"

"I...I can't think of anything." He struggled to get the words out.

"Hey, you wanted this, remember?"

"Yeah, but I didn't know it would hurt this much," he gasped.

The girl laughed. "Why does nobody ever think it will hurt?" She stood up and walked him to the window, then she went and sat down. She leaned back into the sofa and grabbed her bag of popcorn. "It's time. Are you ready?"

He didn't open his eyes, but he nodded.

As the girl watched, his skull separated. Blood, bone, and brain matter sprayed in a crimson dance through the air. She applauded as it struck the perfectly white wall in a Rorschach chart of gore. Smiling, she walked up to the mess as the body began to fall. She picked up a little piece of brain and poked it, gently. It wobbled in her palm. "Hey, mister," she whispered. "Could you feel the wall?"

The piece of brain didn't reply. The girl smiled. "I hope you got what you wanted," she said.

Then she kissed the bit of grey matter, set it back in the pile, and walked away.

The gun went off like a jolt of thunder. In an instant, he was dead.

Timber

Gregor sat in the inn, warming himself by the fire. He watched as the flames danced in hues of orange and blue with every passerby and every opening of the door. After a time, and several pints of stout, he began to fancy that he could see figures in the flames – creatures of heat and light, meeting here, drawn by the presence of their own kind.

The flames danced, and someone sat in the chair opposite to Gregor. A few moments passed, then the newcomer cleared his throat. "Are you alright, boy?" came a rough, though not uncaring voice.

Gregor looked up. Through the spots in his vision, he saw an old man sitting in his stocking feet, smiling at him . "I'm fine," he lied, and turned back to the fire.

The old man took a sip from the cup he held in his lap. "You don't look fine," he started. "In fact, you look like hell."

Gregor didn't look up. "It's been that kind of day," he said, relenting.

The old man nodded, tugging at the straggly, gray strands of hair hanging from his chin. "I know what you need," he said, snapping his fingers. "You need a story! Something to take your mind off your troubles." He took a handful of coal from nearby and threw it into the fire, where it broke, sputtered, and finally caught. "What's more," the old man continued, "you need a true story."

He watched the fire burn for a moment, then took a sip of his drink and turned again to Gregor. "Do you know why we only burn coal in this town?" he asked.

Gregor stirred uncomfortably in his seat. The old man's voice had a taunting quality about it. It carried with it a note of teasing and gloating, as if the knowledge the old man possessed was as simple and as important as the color of the sky or the movement of water, and the fact that Gregor could possibly not know was something to be rightfully ridiculed. He turned to the old man. "No," he said, annoyed.

The old man's smile broadened in a way that seemed to mock Gregor's mood. He signaled to the barmaid to bring him another drink, then put his feet up on a footstool and, when he was comfortable, began.

"You wouldn't think it from the looks of this town, but it is ancient in the extreme. Lots of the buildings have been torn down to be used as the blocks for others, only for those to be torn down in turn. But the town as a whole has been here, in one form or another, for thousands of years.

"And yet, old as it is, the tree that stands not one hundred feet from here is older. One might even say that this town is here because of that tree."

The old man paused to take a long pull from his antique clay mug, then continued.

"It's said that, long ago, a great battle took place here. Some stories say it was men in iron with swords, others say they had only leather and bronze, and some say it was just animal skins and clubs. But however it was fought, one things is certain: it was an absolute bloodbath. By the end, neither side of the conflict could claim victory, and the survivors buried the bodies where they fell.

"And so, whether from a lack of troops or due to the horrors of that battle, a peace was reached. To commemorate that peace, and to honor the dead, a tree was planted where the fighting was thickest. As time went by, and as the tree grew, it carried the bodies and bones of the fallen with it, blending them into its bark and branches. Both sides of the conflict had a severe respect for their fighting dead, and their shared customs demanded that the resting place for them, wherever it was, be guarded from those who would desecrate them. There was only one problem: one skeleton looks much like another, and neither side could say who's dead was who's.

"So another agreement was made – two buildings would be made of stone, each housing the priests from their respective side who would care for the grounds and for the tree that made up the site of the battle. Now, the people in those cottages couldn't farm the land for fear of disrupting their buried dead, so all food was shipped-in to them on carts. Naturally, the area soon became a hub of trade, because where you have men with goods and carts, money follows. The trade post became an inn, the inn required a bar, the bar required a brewery, and, before long, the tree had its own town.

"Of course, time takes its toll on everything, even old traditions and customs, and the battle, the warriors, and the bodies which make up the foundations of this town were eventually forgotten.

"New rulers came and took possession of the town, only to lose it to another in the next war that came through, who lost it in the war after that. Indeed, the town was built on death, and seemed to attract it like a lover. People began to whisper that it was cursed.

"Until some king or lord came and made this place his home. A castle was built, though some say it was a keep, and others a simple hunting lodge. What is agreed is that this ruler kept power with an iron fist, and the lawlessness that sprang up through changing hands so often would not be tolerated. To this end, an execution square was built around the once holy site, and that giant of a tree, with its many thick boughs and sturdy roots, would be used as a gallows..."

The old man paused, looking into his empty mug. Gregor was no longer staring into the fire. Instead, he found himself enveloped by the tale of the city he had always called home. The old man bellowed for another drink, and Gregor asked him what it was he was drinking.

"Oh, you wouldn't like it," he said. "It's an old concoction, and tastes change with time. But where was I? Ah, yes. The gallows...

"Those were dark days for this town. The ruler oversaw each execution personally, delighting in the dance macabre. Some of the town's population fled, others hid, but many, many more were put to death on those strong limbs.

"The lord's favorite way to execute someone, by all accounts, was to place their ankles on an anvil and to strike each of them three times with a smith's hammer. Then, he would let the noose hang low – so low, in fact, that the hanged person's feet could touch the ground, if only they could find purchase on their shattered bones. Those who were still alive after an hour of agony were rewarded by having their bellies split open. Some of the people of the town, poor and in need, began to steal the belongings of the dying as they hung there and struggled for breath. Even a man's shoes weren't safe...'"

He took a long pull of his newly arrived drink before he continued.

"It's said that it was during its time as a gallows that the tree took on the appearance that it still holds today – twisted, black, and seemingly devoid of life.

"Of course, rulers who keep power through death and intimidation tend to meet an unkind end, and it was the same with this one. The townspeople rebelled, the ruler's own soldiers and guards turned on him, and, even as he protested and screamed, they hung him from that ghastly tree. When he didn't die quickly enough, they cut him down, smashed and severed his limbs, and, to stop the screaming, finally slit his throat.

"The ruler's body was sent away, and is said to have been thrown into a lake, and for the first time since its founding, there was peace in the town.

"But people are foolish, and after only a few decades, new fights began. The renaissance had come to the town, and with it came new ways of killing one another. Suddenly, things which were only the fever dreams of the deranged were made into weapons of war for the masses, and though much of the continent had an explosion of science and morality, the people of this town in their houses of stone only discovered that death could now come cheaply.

"Families began to build power for themselves and their blood-line, and through guile and deceit formed petty kingdoms within the town where their word was law. The town itself became divided in three as the people chose sides in the upcoming conflict. The situation was coming to a head. Small-scale battles were breaking out everywhere. So nobody took notice of the single traveler who came into town. Some people say he had boils upon his skin when he arrived, and others say he looked as plain as anyone. He got drunk in this very inn, then went and fell asleep under the tree in the square.

"As he slept, another skirmish erupted from the feuding families and spilled into the square. Whether it was pistol, rapier, pike, or longsword nobody can say, but somehow the stranger was killed as he slept against that tree. His body was pierced right through and pinned to the trunk. The people said that the tree itself bled from the wounds inflicted upon it. After the stranger was buried, people began to notice their own skin boil.

"The plague had come to town."

The old man paused, staring into his cup. When he began once more, his tone was colder.

"It's strange when a once bustling town becomes a ghost of itself – when whole districts go quiet and still as death takes hold. Nobody was safe. The plague killed the old and young, the rich and poor alike. The families in power forgot their feuds as their numbers dwindled, but that didn't save them. In the end, only one in ten survived the black death in this town...

"In the years that followed, life seemed to suddenly be worth more. The old ways were dying without the population to support them, and people took solace in newer religions. The priests who had cared for the tree since time immemorial were wiped out, and all that was left was the discomfort of tradition when people began to dig up the old warriors' bones to till the soil and plant their crops or expand their homes.

"But even if most of the graves had been disturbed, most of the honored dead desecrated, they still would not cut the wood here, lest it hold the vengeance of centuries of dead at its core."

The old man bowed in his chair, his bones popping and creaking with a dull, hollow tone. "Wars came and went after that, but that's another story, and one story was, I think, more than you bargained for," he said, smiling.

The fire had gone low in the telling of the tale, and the hour had grown late. Gregor thanked the old man for the story, then left the warmth of the pub and entered the blood-chilling cold of winter. He turned up his collar to the wind and pulled a cigarette from his pocket. He closed his eyes to the blinding flame as he lit it and took a lungful of smoke.

He breathed it out again as he looked at the ancient hanging tree, dead to its core, and he wondered if it had ever been alive at all, or if it had simply survived off of the doomed residents of the town since it was planted – keeping enough of them alive to sustain it in times of need.

He walked up to the trunk, staring into the branches and bark, wondering if the dead that time had forgotten were watching him in return. He looked over the vines that snaked up this wooden corpse like the remnants of every rope that had ever been used to hang the condemned, and maybe, he thought, they were what they seemed.

He took another drag on his cigarette and exhaled, watching the smoke float up through the branches and pass by the oddly comforting shape of a noose that he had tied to a sturdy branch hours before. He sighed, then smiled. He was about the dash out the embers of his cigarette on the trunk of the tree, but halted. Instead, he lifted his boot and put it out on his heel, then turned and walked away. Looking back over his shoulder, he could have sworn he saw the old man grinning at him from somewhere in the bark, but then, that could have been his imagination.

159

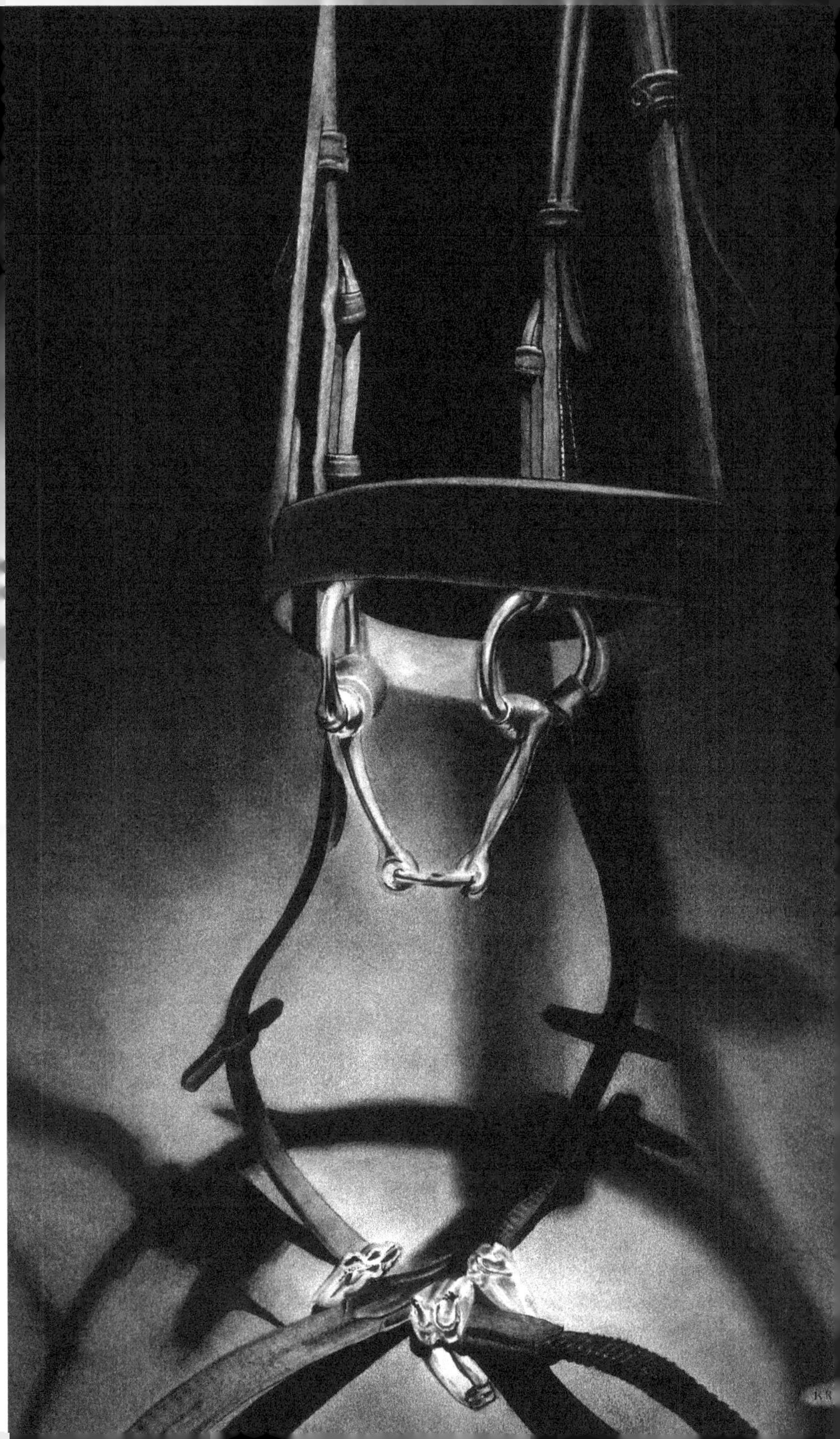

To Catch a Kelpie

It was a pleasant day for a walk. That is to say, as pleasant as a day can get in springtime, in the valley, in Scotland. It was raining, which was to be expected, but the sun was out, which was not. Mollie walked along a river that twisted and turned its way along the valley floor, etching itself into the slate and rocky soil through nothing more than stubborn determination.

Mollie generally approved of rivers. Others living in the nearby village said they were dangerous, that they attracted beasts and flooded without warning, but Mollie had lived near to this river all her life, and the only beasts she'd ever seen were a sickly wolf and a deer. Animals didn't tend to venture too close to the village. They had learned better. But, it would seem, not all of them.

Up ahead, a horse splashed along in the shallows, kicking up great sprays of water and then running through them. It whinnied and played, and Mollie watched, fascinated.

She had never owned a horse. Her family had been poor when they were alive, and they were poorer still now that sickness had claimed most of them. The remaining members lived far from the village, if they still lived at all.

The horse stopped, having spotted Mollie staring at it. She took a step forward and the horse immediately bolted away down the shoreline. Mollie sighed, disenchanted, and returned home.

The sun was setting when she reached her empty hovel. She set to work on her evening meal, boiling what vegetables were left in her larder. That night, she dreamed of horses, of riding on their backs, the wind blowing through her hair as they wove through the forest trails. She had never known such speeds, nor such fun.

The next morning, Mollie skipped her chores and went back to the river, determined to experience her dream in reality. She reached the same spot she had seen the horse in less than an hour, but nothing was there today. Undeterred, she pressed on, further upstream.

She'd never been this far from home, before. The river's course lead her into a small woodland, and a short time later she began to hear the roar of a waterfall. The forest parted, and ahead of her stood a great cliff face. The river fell from its source somewhere high in the mountains, and into a basin here in the woods, forming a large pool. But Mollie hadn't noticed any of that. Her eyes were focused on the large creature standing just inside the pool.

It looked like a horse in basic shape, but it was larger, its long mane was speckled here and there with moss, and where most wild horses were afraid of humans, this one seemed calm and content. It looked at Mollie, then walked forward off of the rocky shore and in reach of the grass nearby. It bent down and started eating, never taking its eye off of her.

Mollie carefully approached, taking each step as softly as she could so as not to startle the creature. It stopped eating and turned to face her, staring her straight in the eye.

Why am I being so cautious? Mollie thought. Standing up straight, she walked to the massive beast directly, and it did not retreat. It simply watched her, staring into her. Mollie reached out to stroke its huge muzzle. She touched it...

...and her hand stayed in place, as if glued to the creature's skin. She tried to pull away, but it was like she were pulling her own body – like they were fused. The great horse shook its head and nearly broke Mollie's arm off. Slowly, carefully, it turned around and started walking, forcing Mollie backward into the freezing pool.

The water was past her shins. In a panic, she kicked at the creature with her simple shoes, but it moved on as if it hadn't noticed. The water was up to her stomach, and she screamed, trying to pull her own arm away from her body, to separate her skin and sinew by force and by will. The water was at her neck, and she spotted something metallic under the beasts long mane: a bridle. She reached for it with her free hand just as her head went under.

NO!

The waterfall, so loud in the open air, sounded almost hollow from beneath the water. Mollie opened her eyes in the murky liquid, The creature had stopped walking. She looked above her. The open air was only a few inches away, but she was still stuck fast to the creature's muzzle.

Her lungs ached. She turned the creature's head using the hand that held the bridle, and the creature allowed its head to be moved. She tried pushing it backward, forcing it out of the water, but she had no leverage here, nothing to brace herself on. Her body cried out for air.

Move, damn you! she thought in frustration, and the creature turned, and began walking out of the water.

Mollie breached into the open air with a gasp, taking great gulps of breath. The creature kept walking out of the pool and onto the shore, dragging Mollie along as she coughed and sputtered. She pushed on the bridle, and the creature stopped.

Let me go. The voice entered her mind, uninvited and unwelcome. The creature stared at Mollie.

"Is that you?" she asked.

Let me go, the voice repeated.

"Give me back my hand," Mollie demanded, and suddenly her hand was free. She pulled it away and let it hang at her side, her shoulder protesting every movement. She looked at the bridle in her other hand, and something occurred to her. "You have to do as I say while I'm holding onto this, don't you?"

The creature stared at her, but didn't respond.

"Alright," Mollie said, pondering. "Back up three steps." The creature backed away, and Mollie followed pace. She laughed. "Very well, then, listen to me. You are never to harm me, ever again. Is that understood?"

Yes.

"And you will obey that command?"

Yes.

"Good. Now..." She looked around for a rock she could use as a stepping stone. "Something else I need from you."

It was sunset when she returned home. She sat atop the creature, riding far forward to avoid letting go of the bridle, but Mollie was smiling.

It had been better than it was in her dreams. The creature never seemed to tire, and it reached speeds a normal horse would never be able to match. They had ridden for hours, visiting places Mollie had only ever heard of.

A thought struck her. "What will happen when I let go of the bridle?"

I will leave, and return to the river, the creature replied.

"To try to find others to kill?"

Yes.

"And what if I command you not to leave? Will you have to stay?" The creature didn't answer, and Mollie smiled. "It is so ordered, then. When I let go of your bridle, you will stay exactly where you are until I come back for you again."

The creature shook its head in annoyance.

"Will you do as I command?" Mollie asked.

Yes.

"Good." She let go of the bridle and slid down off the creature's back, rolling when she hit the ground. She stood up and looked to make sure it hadn't run off, but there it was, staring at her with its massive eyes, as if bored, and frustrated, and humiliated.

Mollie backed into her hovel, keeping the creature in sight. Before she closed the door, she smiled at the creature. "Goodnight," she said, sweetly.

The creature glared as Mollie shut the door.

The next day, Mollie awoke and rushed outside. The creature still stood where she had left it, and it had eaten a circle in the grass around itself. The bare patch of earth was slowly turning to mud in the rain.

"Ah," Mollie said, having the good sense to look ashamed. "Sorry. I... forgot you might want to eat."

The creature rolled its eyes.

They spent that day plowing the area around Mollie's hovel in preparation for planting. The great strength of the creature made quick work of the soil, and with its help she was able to plant enough that season to sell excess crops to the village.

Before long, rumors started to spread about the strange woman who lived near the river, and of her hulking giant of a horse. The rumors turned cruel when someone overheard her speaking to it.

"She's a witch," they would say. "She enchanted her lover and he became the horse that she is never seen without!"

As the rumors spread, Mollie went to the village less and less.

Humans are strange, the creature said one evening. Mollie had given it free reign at night to do as it pleased, so long as it would be in front of her door every morning. Some nights, it chose to stay and keep her company.

"Yes, we are," Mollie admitted.

Let me go. Perhaps you can still salvage your reputation.

Mollie looked out of her door at the creature standing there. Though it had been years since they met, it hadn't grown a day older, and it had lost none of its ire in all that time, even refusing to take a name, saying that names were human things, and thus not to be trusted.

"I can't," Mollie replied. "Who would I talk to if I did?"

She smiled at the creature, and, she thought, it was pleased.

Time passed. Every few years, someone from the village would risk visiting the witch to know things that they shouldn't know about lovers or about trade items from neighboring towns, or to ask revenge on someone who had wronged them, and in that way Mollie found purpose. The creature knew things that no human could possibly know, and was formidable when allowed to be, and on more than one occasion she asked its help in dealing with what she called 'local problems.'

In her twilight years, Mollie had become part of the village legends, as much as the blacksmith who fathered twenty children or the cow who bore only two-headed calves. It became common to blame The Witch of the River for bad happenings, and to thank her for random good fortune.

Mollie knew something was brewing in the village. It was only a matter of time before something big would happen, and she would get the blame.

It was after a particularly fearsome season that she was proved correct. The drought had killed many of the crops that the village needed to survive, and when the rain finally did come, landslides destroyed several homes. It was even said that the coming war with the English was all due to the witch and her sorcery.

And so they came one night with torches and picks, with hoes and pitchforks, and burned the witch's hovel to the ground.

They never found body nor bone of her or her beast in the ruins, and there were some who said that the witch had planned this all along, but, by and large, they were certain that the deed was done.

To this very day, every so often, travelers tell of the kindly old woman who offered to take them across the river on the back of her great horse, and how lucky they were to have found her. And every now and then, someone from the village will vanish for weeks, only for their battered body to wash up on the river's shore.

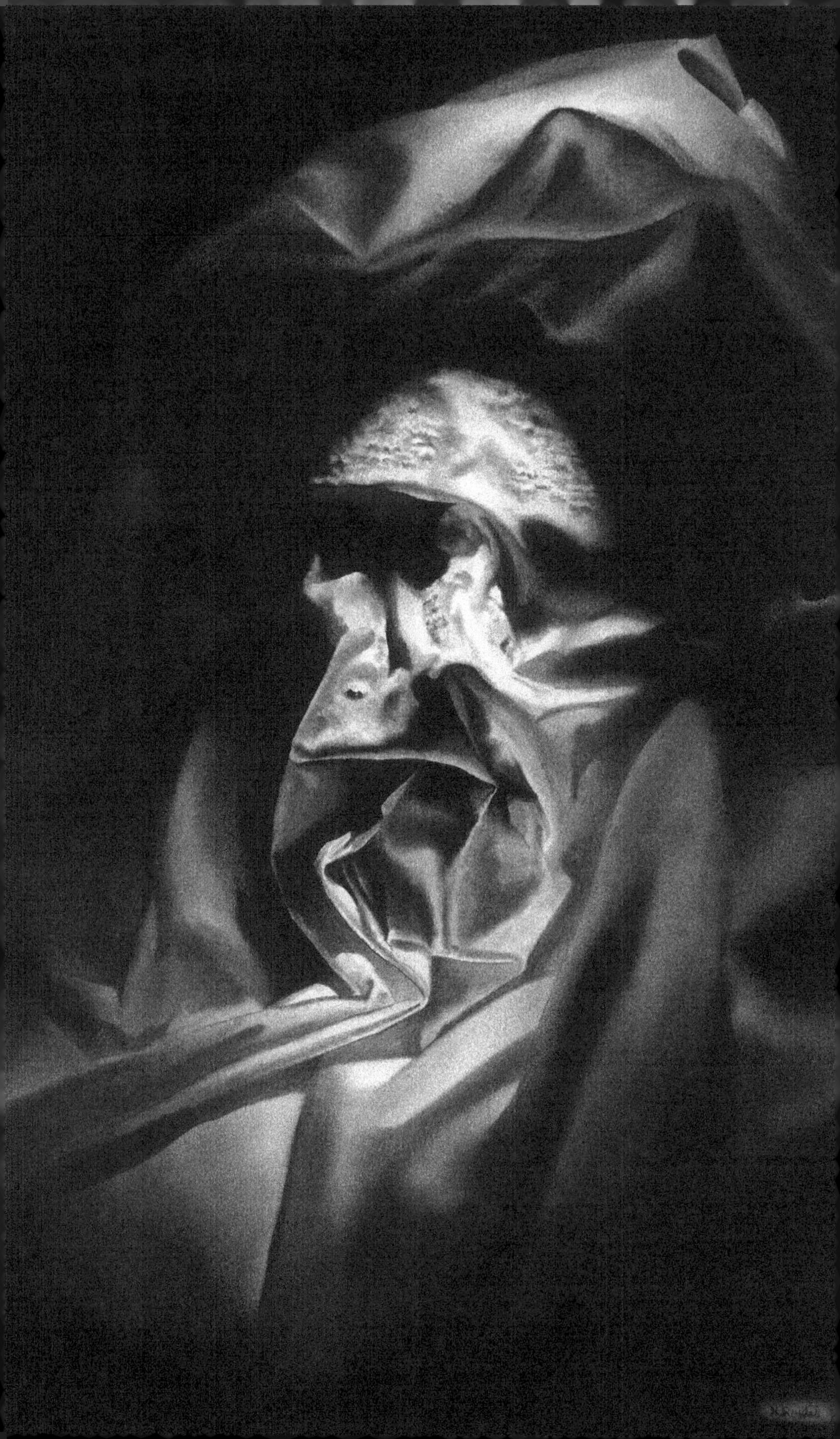

Unconscious Mistakes

Sleep – the calm, relaxing tranquility. A cessation of function to rebuild, recharge, and decompress.

And to dream.

But to Frederick, sleep was just a prelude to terror. Every night, try as he might, he woke up screaming from a deep, deep slumber. He had taken to warning lovers and neighbors that it would happen, to not be alarmed at any shrieks they might hear in the night, and that it was something he was trying to fix.

And indeed, he was trying to fix it.

Doctor Stein sat behind his desk, looking at the proceedings with a kind of bemused grin. Frederick was lying on a sofa, watching a small, silver ball roll back and forth in Doctor Smith's hand. She was saying something about listening to her voice, the tone, the timbre of it, but Frederick wasn't paying attention. He was too busy looking at her thumb.

It was a bit mutilated, but it didn't appear to be from injury or mutation. The flesh was puckered, baring prominent teeth marks all along the inside. *Stress,* Frederick thought, finally turning his attention back to the doctor's voice.

"When you wake up from a nightmare, you won't scream. What you will do is pay very close attention to your surroundings. Observe every minute detail so that we can further explore what it is that's terrifying you," she said, still rolling the silver ball back and forth.

Frederick stared at it, trying to ignore Doctor Smith's thumb as he did. He found himself quite relaxed, now. Something about her voice seemed soothing to his chaotic mind.

"Is this really going to work?" he heard Doctor Stein ask, realizing for the first time that he had closed his eyes.

"It will if he lets it," replied Doctor Smith.

And then Frederick shuffled off into oblivion.

Frederick awoke to an overwhelming sense of cold. The air that wafted through the room felt to him like invisible icebergs, slowly grinding down his skin, exposing raw nerves. He opened his eyes, and proceeded to panic. He couldn't move. He was seemingly frozen in place, as if his mind had awoken but his body hadn't gotten the message.

The doctors were talking to one another, but they sounded quiet, distant.

"Should we wake him?" one asked.

"Nah, let him sleep. He doesn't get enough as it is," the other replied.

Frederick tried to force himself to move, but it was hopeless. His limbs were dead weight hanging from a lifeless torso. *Am I still asleep?* he thought, watching the doctors banter. *Did I just forget to close my eyes?*

Something in Doctor Smith's hand caught his eye. A small creature, no larger than a hamster, crawled out of her sleeve and gently began gnawing at her thumb. She scratched at her thumb with her pointer finger and it moved aside, and then went right back to work. It spotted Frederick in mid-chew, a tiny spec of flesh still hanging from its chin.

It smiled at him.

Books, giant medical tomes, began to work their way out of the bookshelf behind the doctors. First one, then another, then a third. It was as if something was pushing the volumes forward on the shelf. The creature in Doctor Smith's hand noticed, and climbed back up her sleeve.

The unseen something worked its way up the shelf. When it hit the wall, Frederick could almost make out its shape in the shifting plaster and paint, tunneling through from somewhere outside of reality. The doctors were oblivious, even when feet not unlike those of a man pressed themselves out of the wall, and began walking against gravity, step by step.

Frederick lost sight of it as it reached the ceiling. When it didn't reappear after several minutes, he breathed a mental sigh of relief. That was when something brushed against him from the wall behind the sofa. Frederick shifted his gaze to the extreme side, and there he saw it, claws imbedded in stretched plaster and paint, blurred by the extremity of his peripheral vision. Something began to tear behind him, and for a moment, he thought he heard it breathing.

Doctor Stein gently shook Frederick by the shoulder, who immediately shot off the sofa and landed on the floor. He coughed and gasped, taking in air as if he hadn't breathed since falling asleep.

"Did you see it?" he choked between breaths.

But Doctor Stein only looked at him with confusion and concern, not fear. Frederick gathered his wits and stood up, unsure of what to say or how to begin. Doctor Stein smiled at him. "Time's up for this week," he said, "but I expect to know how things go with your night terrors when I see you next."

Doctor Smith walked forward and offered her hand to Frederick by way of goodbye, but he just stood there, starring at her thumb, and the fresh dot of blood drying in the draft.

"I'll uh... I'll see you next week," he said, and tried not to run as he hurried out the door.

That night found him lying in bed, staring at the ceiling, once again unable to sleep. He tried counting sheep, picturing them jumping a small fence one-by-one. When he had counted three hundred, he looked around inside his sleep-deprived world at all of the woolen-coated creatures, standing around, surrounding him as he counted. He looked into their oblong irises, stared at three hundred sets of them, all watching him as if demanding to know why they had been summoned.

He opened his eyes. Sheep were definitely out.

Hours passed. He tossed and turned and found he was unable to get comfortable. He thought about drinking a glass of warm milk, but there are some things even the most desperate of people will not do.

Finally, the grey of dawn appeared outside his window, banishing the darkness by inches, and he finally felt comfortable. As drowsiness overtook him, he fell asleep.

The next day was, to his delight, uninteresting. He didn't wake up screaming. He went to work, spent a lot of his time messing around at his computer, ate lunch, did virtually nothing afterward, and went home. He was beginning to think that he was having an uncharacteristically good day.

"No, you're not," said the sheep standing in his dining room.

Frederick opened his eyes. It was morning, and the sun filtered in through his blinds, giving the room a soft light. *Damn,* he thought, as he tried to move and found that he was unable to. He felt restrained, somehow. It was as if the blanket on top of him was made of lead and held him in place.

Somewhere in the house, there grew a hissing.

He watched the carpet get stretched and pulled as something crawled toward him from underneath, distorting the world as it moved. It slid across the floor, up his bed frame, and along his blanket. It twisted and moved, forming a face in the cloth. It reached up with its clawed hands, and grabbed at the stretched reality in front of it. Slowly, it pulled, and as a tear formed, Frederick saw what it was that had been stalking him.

And he remembered seeing it countless times before. Every night when he woke, when the barriers between what was real and what was imagined were thinnest, his stalker would arrive from the other side.

And he would scream, sending it scurrying back from whence it came.

Every night.

By the gods, how he wished that he could scream.

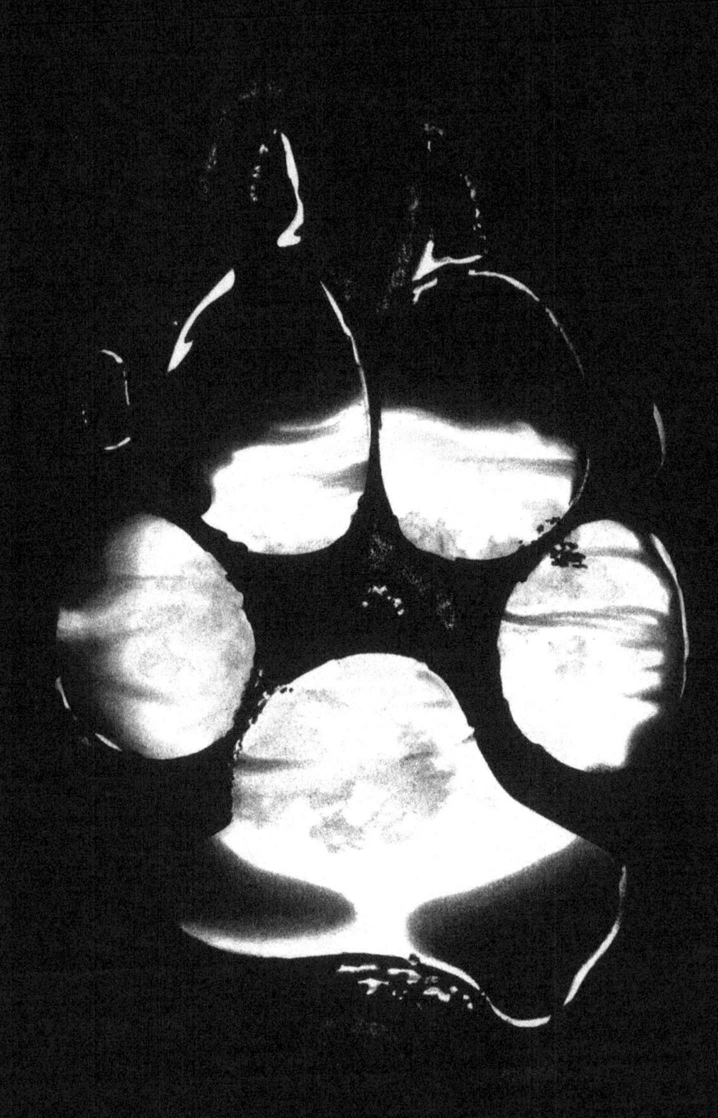

Instinct

It happened on accident. Luna was simply walking home one night after work, minding her own business, when the hair on the back of her neck stood on end. She walked faster down the narrow streets and corridors, unsure if she was simply letting her imagination run away with her.

When she reached a blind corner, she went around it, ducked behind a hedgerow, and waited. A few moments passed. She was just beginning to feel a little silly when she saw it.

It was massive. Patches of bristly fur stood out against the moonlight as it turned the corner, and with each step, great claws gripped and cut into the concrete. It alternated walking like a man and being down on all four limbs as it paused to sniff the air. Luna gasped when the creature turned and looked directly at her, hidden behind the hedgerow. It growled, deep and long, and she found herself frozen in place.

Just as it seemed the beast was going to pounce, it turned. A man and his dog had rounded the corner. The tiny pug was barking at the beast, pulling its dumbfounded person forward against his will.

Then the beast leapt.

The pug continued to bark and snarl and bite at the beast as the beast ripped the man to pieces. Finally annoyed, the beast growled at the pug, who turned and ran.

Luna came to her senses just as the beast began to feast. She ran as fast as she could, all the way to her flat a mile away.

She turned and locked the door, latched the chain, and pressed her back against it. As soon as she caught her breath, she screamed.

It was a week later, when she began to see missing person fliers posted around town of the man she had seen eaten, that she finally decided she wasn't crazy. She had seen that beast kill a man. A beast that could only have been a werewolf. But what could she do? Report it to the police and hope that they didn't lock her up? And how was it they didn't discover the man's body? Surely there must have at least been pieces left behind.

Luna began to study up on werewolf lore, digging into the oldest references she could, trying to make sense of it all. She went to the spot where the man had been killed, but the whole area had been repaired and repainted. The neighbors said someone had struck an animal with their car, and that nothing but gore had remained of the poor creature.

She had run out of ideas. *Even if they think I'm crazy,* she decided, *I must tell the police what I've seen.*

The next day, she woke up early to go to the police station. On the way, she stopped at a café and got a rather large cup of coffee, more to give her courage than energy. As she left the café into the brisk morning air, she saw something that caught her attention – it was the dead man's pug, and it was sitting under the table of a young man who was nose-deep in a laptop.

The dog growled at her when it noticed her standing there for too long, but went silent at a whisper from the man. He looked up at Luna and smiled.

"I'm sorry about him. He's been through a lot lately, and it's left him a bit leery of strangers."

Luna stood there a moment too long, motionless, staring.

"Are you okay?" the man asked.

"Um... what?" Luna stammered.

"You're just kind of standing there, staring at me. Are you okay?"

"Oh! Sorry. Yes, I'm fine. It's just been a long day."

The man glanced at his laptop. "It's 9am," he said, flatly.

"I, uh... I work nights. So... almost bed time for me."

The man stared back at her. "Okay, then. Well... goodnight?"

"Right... right! Sorry, I'm just... I'll go. Nice meeting you."

"Likewise," the man smiled, managing to hide that he must think Luna's out of her mind.

Luna walked back down the street in a daze, heading back toward her flat. She was halfway there when she stopped in her tracks. *Shit!* she thought, and ran back to the café.

She got back just as the man was getting ready to leave. She ducked into a store entrance and peered around the corner, watching him. When he started to walk away, she followed. She felt obvious and pretentious, as if she were in a bad comedy and the whole world could see that she was following the handsome man with the dog, but nobody stopped her or asked why she kept dodging behind parked cars, or why she couldn't seem to keep a steady walking pace.

Finally, the man went into an apartment building, across the street from a disused, overgrown park surrounded by an iron fence. Luna stood outside for several minutes, wondering if she should go in after him, but she thought better of it. Somehow, walking into a stranger's apartment and accusing them of being a werewolf didn't seem to be a sensible plan.

Besides, she thought, *I don't know if he's a werewolf, yet.* She pulled out her phone and noted down the building address, and then she went home to plan.

Luna spent much of the next week sitting in the same café that she'd seen the man in, trying to manufacture a spontaneous meeting. She thought that if she could somehow sit down with him and get him to talk, that she might find something that would prove he was a wolf in man's clothing.

He walked into the café after dark, just a few minutes before closing. She observed him, trying to notice anything odd about his movements, his mannerisms, but if there was anything odd about him, she couldn't see it.

She walked over to him while he waited for his coffee. "Excuse me," she said, smiling.

He turned to her. "Yes?" Then he pointed at her. "Oh, hey, aren't you-"

"The weird woman who stared at you until you got uncomfortable the other day?" she finished for him. "Yep, that's me."

He laughed. "That's not exactly how I would have put it," he said, smiling. "Are you feeling better?"

Has he always had such a nice smile? she thought. Out loud, she said "Oh, yeah. Loads better, thank you."

"Good. Had me worried there for a moment." The barista delivered his coffee to him, thanked him, and left. "Well," he said, grabbing his coffee, "it was nice seeing you again, uh…"

"Luna," said Luna.

"Really? Huh. Well, it was nice seeing you again, Luna." he nodded to her and held out his free hand. "My name is David."

They shook. David was already headed out the door when Luna called after him. "I don't suppose you'd want to go get dinner someplace?" she asked.

David paused in the doorway. "What, now?"

"Yeah, unless you're not hungry."

David smiled. "I could eat a horse," he said, holding the door open for her. Luna really wished he hadn't put it quite like that.

They went to a restaurant nearby and made small talk over their food. "Where's your little dog tonight?" Luna asked, stabbing a bit of broccoli with her fork.

"Oh, he's at home. He doesn't like going out with me after dark for some reason," David replied, slicing into a rare cut of beef. Luna watched the blood pool on his plate, watched it ooze from the meat. Her memory flashed back to the man who died that night. "This steak is fantastic," David said, cutting another slice. "Would you like to try it?"

Luna fought back the urge to vomit. "No, thank you," she said, trying not to retch. "I recently became a vegetarian."

"Really?" David popped the morsel of barely cooked flesh into his mouth. "I'm sorry, I didn't know." He called the waiter over and asked for a small box. He then slid the meat into the box and closed it. "There," he said, smiling." No sense in you being uncomfortable over dinner."

Luna smiled. "So, what brought you to the café so late in the day?" she asked.

"You're all sorts of nosy, aren't you?" David teased.

"Well, I am out to dinner with an almost complete stranger."

"Yeah, but it was your idea."

Luna shrugged in response.

David laughed. 'I just never really seem to get much sleep, that's all. I have the most bizarre dreams all night long, and I wake up tired."

"What kind of dreams?" Luna pressed.

"Just random nonsense, really. Anyway, how's your dinner?"

The rest of dinner went exceedingly well, and David offered to walk Luna home. They stood in front of her flat, holding hands. "Thank you for inviting me out," David said, smiling. "But I could have paid my end."

"I invited you, remember? Next time, you can invite me, and then you can pay." Luna returned his smile.

"I don't know. I might be spoiled, now. Free food and good company? I think I could get used to that."

Luna pulled her hand away from his, pretending to be mad, then tried to slap him on the shoulder. David avoided her swing, caught her by the waist, pulled her close, and kissed her.

Luna pulled away first. "Do you think that dog of yours can look after itself for the night?" She asked, hopefully.

"I think he would understand," David whispered, and they both went into the flat together.

They slept late, lying in each other's arms for what seemed like forever. Eventually, David got out of bed and got dressed. "I think my dog will be quite angry with me when I get home," he said, pulling his t-shirt on. His head popped out the top and he saw Luna stretching out on the bed in a yawn, still nude. "Definitely worth it, though," he added.

Luna threw a pillow at his head, and they laughed. "I'll see you tonight?" she asked.

David stopped and thought for a moment. "Maybe. I might be busy, but give me a call. Maybe I can cook for you if I'm free."

They kissed their goodbyes, and he left.

Luna took a nap. When she awoke, she took a shower and got dressed. It was already evening by the time she left the house. She went to the café for a sandwich and coffee, dreading work the next day. She pulled out her phone and was about to text David, but then she remembered that his place was only a couple blocks away, and decided she would surprise him, confront him with what she knew already, and tell him that she wanted to help him.

The sun fell while she ate. She walked to David's apartment by lamplight, wondering if it were prudent, wondering if she was being a fool.

She got to the building before she realized that she still had no idea which apartment was his. She thought of a plan to mess with him – she would stand across the street and call him, tell him to go to the window, and then wave at him. She could always excuse away how she knew where he lived.

So, she crossed the street, standing in front of an iron fence. The bushes beyond the fence were massive, and Luna wondered when the city would trim them. She pulled out her phone and called David.

The phone rang, on and on, until it went to voicemail. Luna sighed and tried again. Again, it went to voicemail. She was just beginning to write him a text when she heard the snap of a branch behind her, and a low, guttural growl she'd only ever heard once before.

The next day, David awoke in his own bed. He had fallen asleep early the night before, but the strange dreams and nightmares he always had meant that he was still exhausted. He sat up. A wet chewing noise was coming from under the bed.

David rolled onto his stomach and peered over the edge of the bed to see his new pug delightedly chewing on somebody's arm. The dog pulled back and gave a tiny bark, its face covered in gore, and it wagged its tail. David followed the arm with his eyes until he spotted the head. He recognized her.

"Ugh. Not again," he said, lying back on the bed and sighing. "She seemed really nice."

And then, yawning, David went back to sleep.

FRANKENSTEIN
K.Ruggles

<u>The Creature's Lament</u>

My dear brother Ivan,

I hope this letter finds you well. Do your studies proceed? I admit, the thought of you being so far from home fills me with dread, but we shall be here still when you return. As for me, I have a story to relate.

The strangest occurrence preceded the dawn. In the night, I awoke to horrified shrieks coming from the stable. Thinking it thieves after my stud stock, I grabbed my rifle and ran out in my nightgown ready to fire at anyone I came across. Reaching the stables, I threw the door open and thrust my torch into the darkness. The horses were all against the corner to my left, and (to my horror) my prize stud lay dead beneath the shod hooves of his colts.

They trod on him still. Even as I tried to calm them, they pummeled him into the dirt, trying to climb the walls to get away from whatever was kneeling at the other end of the stable. The shrouded figure was layered in a thick great coat and had a strange hide over his shoulders and head. The man, for it must have been a man, was huddled over another figure in the darkness.

I raised my rifle, but before I could issue my warnings, the figure spoke. "You could do me no greater kindness than to end my wretched existence." His voice was as cold as the north winds, but gentle like the new dawn.

The man's eloquent speech and shambled appearance confounded me, brother, and I stayed my hand from the judgment I was ready to administer. "Who are you?" I cried. "What are you doing here?"

The man stood, unfolding his great and powerful body. He was a full eight feet tall, but any detail in his face remained shrouded in the shadow of the hides he wore. Behind him lay a pile of rags that may have been a rucksack or something more sinister. The giant rumbled, "I am lost! So... so very lost."

"If you are lost, why did you not come to the house?" I asked. The fright in my horses still worried me.

"I would not be welcome in your, or any, house," he replied. The tone and timbre of his sad voice made me not question his resolve.

I attempted to move closer to the man, if man he was, but he backed away and shouted "Stay your place!" His words echoed in the stable like thunder in the hills.

"Who are you?" I asked him when I had regained my wits.

"A coward, or nothing at all," he responded, quietly.

"How could one such as you be a coward?" I balked at him.

He motioned to the bundle I had mistaken for rags. "That was my father," he said. "He followed me from Geneva into the cold wastes of the north, chasing me, wanting to destroy me. But the journey proved too much for his delicate and temperate frame. He expired among the sailors of a northern expedition vessel." The giant sighed. "I couldn't even kill him myself. I hated him, and I loved him; I admired his brilliance, and I despised his disaffection. I am a coward." He hung his great head in shame, in the shadows at the other end of the stable.

"What wrong could your father have committed against you that you would want him dead?" I asked. I admit, this man intrigued me, brother. There was something otherworldly about him—something macabre and enchanting.

"He created me, and he abandoned me," he replied. "He could not stand the sight of me."

Then I thought I understood. His father had sired a bastard, a shame to his family, and would not claim him as his own. I felt pity for this man. I could not help it. "How is it that you came to have your father's body?" I pressed further, wondering at the corpse that must be, even now, decomposing under the rags.

"I had left the sailors behind, consigned and content with my fate among the frozen wastes. But, as I was drifting away, I heard a funeral dirge, and I knew they would soon be giving my father a burial at sea. I came back in time to see them thrust his lifeless husk overboard, and I dove into the chilled depths after him." He turned, then, to the rags. "He deserves better," he finished, sadly.

I eased my way closer to him and, in his grief and misery, he took no notice.

He continued. "I promised the captain of that ship that I would form my own pyre to throw myself upon, but I couldn't even do that. The wood refused to burn – a punishment for my cowardice." He didn't turn to me. I was finally close enough to cast a glare from my torch upon the body at the giant's feet, and it revealed him. The dead man was pale and sickly in appearance. His beard was full of ice and frozen dirt. I knelt down next to him to check for life, but no steam escaped his blue lips. And still the giant didn't stir.

"What will you do?" I asked him, standing once again.

"I will bury him in hallowed ground, as a god deserves."

"And then?"

But what he may have said or done, I will never know, for at that moment he looked up from his personal reverie and turned toward the torch.

His face, brother, was a patchwork of scars and old stitches. His arm flew with inhuman speed and struck the torch from my hand. At his sudden violence, I fired my rifle – forgotten but ready. He screamed in rage.

The torch landed in the hay nearby and began a blaze, driving the creature to further anger. He threw me, bodily, across the stable, and I must admit, brother, that I fell unconscious.

I awoke to a holocaust, the giant and the body were gone, but as I left the stable I heard screams of anguish on the wind, and I knew one thing for certain: the creature was alive. He was most assuredly alive.

I tried to track him this morning, but the snowfall obliterated any trace of his passing, save for the ruin of our stable and the loss of my prized stud.

I hope London treats you well. Father sends his love, and mother begs that I ask if you've found anyone special in that strange city. For myself, I just hope that you've not encountered anything like that creature in your journey.

Your loving brother,
Mikhail

Dearest Mother

I have the most extraordinary tale. The ordeal ended not yet an hour ago, and my hands still tremble as I write this letter. May my soul hold out until I can finish it. By the gods, I cannot seem to catch my breath!

Yesterday, as I completed my mail run to the authorities in the port town of Rostock, I was told that I would have a passenger for my trip back to Hamburg. I should have seen the fear in the man, the anxiety in him, but the road had been harsh, the winter was cruel, and I admit I had taken more than my usual amount of gin to brace me from the cold, so I took no notice. I took my meal and listened to the sailors in the pub. It seemed a newly arrived ship from Russia had been plagued by some sort of ghost, and three young men had been found dead without wounds. I thought nothing of it at the time.

My passenger, it seemed, was a poor, great beast of a man. How he managed to pay for his journey I know not, but my fee was waiting for me upon the mail desk when I prepared to leave an hour after my conversation. My passenger waited for me on a nearby bench, his large sack of possessions clutched in his great hands. I presented myself to him, informing him of the travel time to Hamburg and the conditions, and jesting that the cold had at least driven away the highwaymen that usually plagued this route and had recently claimed the life of my partner.

My passenger made no reply. I reached out to shake his hand and he recoiled as if I had offered the barrel of a rifle. He kept his great head covered, shaded from the light in what looked as if it might have once been sailcloth, crudely stitched together with cord through roughly cut holes, and I began to wonder if this man had been a sailor who was abandoning his ship. Such occurrences are no rarity in Rostock, and a man of his bulk would certainly be worth his feed on a ship of war.

I lead the man out to the mail coach, offering to take his bundle and stow it with the rest of the large packages in the rear netting, and that's when he turned to me…

Mother, perhaps it was the light, perhaps it was the gin, but the look in his eyes seemed colder than the air around me. In a voice like hellfire, he told me that the sack would be riding next to him for the duration of the journey. His tone indicated that refusal was not an option, and seeing his hand upon the sack, I swear that it was larger than the breadth of my chest. Seeing no other option, I opened the door for the man, wondering if the springs would support him. The coach leaned and the tongue groaned as he centered himself within, but they held. How I wish that they had not. The sun was setting as we left Rostock, my fresh team of six anxious to be underway. We made good time despite the heavy cargo we carried. We made the first leg of the journey without incident. We changed horses and were once again underway, my passenger having no wish to relieve himself nor eat while we were stopped. I assumed that the master of his ship must have long arms if my passenger was this far from port and still unable to relax, but who am I to fault a man fleeing that press-ganged life of torment at sea?

It was at least eight hours into our journey when I started to hear something over the rushing wind and through the stout scarf you knit me closed fast around my ears. It was a voice, it seemed to me. Curious, I slowed the horses to hear it better, carefully, easily, so as not to alarm my passenger. "Father," he said, to whom I do not know "why did you create me if not to love me? What I have done to you I have done in rage, and it was less than that which you did to me. Nonetheless, I ask your forgiveness." If he continued speaking afterwards, I did not hear it, but a moment later I heard great sobs coming from the coach – sobs that threatened to rend my heart from my chest from the pain in them. And then he howled like a madman in the darkness, his grief fighting against and overpowering the wind. I drew my scarf closer to my ears to stifle the sound and drove the team onward as fast as they would carry me into the darkness.

A few hours later, a short distance from Hamburg and as the sky was just beginning to lighten, I spotted a man up ahead in the fog and pre-dawn gloom. He raised a gloved hand from his riding cloak and hailed me. I admit my foolishness, but I was compelled to slow if only for the reassurance of another human being, my passenger had un-nerved me so. As soon as I drew the team to a stop, the man reached into his cloak and presented a pistol. I cursed myself as he spoke his threats. Two other men emerged from the side of the road and roughly escorted me off the coach, threatening to shoot me if I struggled. The man who had hailed me peered beyond the lanterns and into the compartment.

"Get out of there!" he demanded of my passenger, either not seeing the bulk of who he was addressing or emboldened by his pistol.

"I have no possessions for you," my passenger said, his voice as black as the darkness that enveloped him. "I wish only to continue my journey. Leave me in peace."

"Are you deaf?! I said get out of there!" The highwayman presented his pistol and reached into the coach to grab my passenger's sack of possessions.

And that was his very last mistake.

In a flash, a fist like the hand of god shot out from the darkness and struck the highwayman. I heard a loud, wet crack that must have been the man's chest and, I fancied, his spine breaking in two. He fell backward to the ground holding where he had been struck, gasping for air like a fish pulled from the sea. The other highwaymen began firing their pistols blindly into the darkness of the coach. I ran from the road and to the safety of a nearby tree. And then I heard it.

Mother, I swear to you this is true. I had consumed no spirits on the return journey, and though I had not slept, I swear it is no delusion. The passenger screamed with a rage unlike any I have ever heard, and as I watched, the coach was lifted wholly into the air and thrown at the two remaining highwaymen as they looked on in shock. The force of the throw knocked my team of six to the ground. Mother, that coach must have weighed over two hundred stone! And the horses must at least have weighed eighty stone each! And yet my passenger treated it as if it were but a mild inconvenience.

The mail coach crushed the two would-be thieves and shattered into kindling. The horses, mangled and shrieking, tried to run, dragging the bodies of those who could not stand and the remains of the hitching equipment into the fog.

I hid behind the tree, praying to the almighty that my passenger might not see me and continue his wrath, and to my everlasting joy, a moment later I heard him taking great steps toward Hamburg.

Mother, I am convinced that I have taken the devil himself as passenger. What other explanation could there be? God knows what would have happened to me if I had delivered this man with the mail coach. I have told no-one else about this, and I will be leaving here tomorrow for Berlin. Nobody would believe what I have seen, and I cannot explain to them within reason what kind of accursed creature I had traveling with me, and that I have delivered into their midst.

Do not think me mad, mother, I beg you. I will write you again when I arrive in Berlin.

Your loving son,

Hans

February the 23rd, 1797

I have long worked in this graveyard. Its stones and monuments, the ghosts and wails of the dearly departed are all old friends of mine. I have received many people attempting to steal the bodies of the freshly dead to sell to the men of medicine here in Geneva, and I have chased out those who failed to meet my price by the tip of my spade. Never in all my long years here have I ever seen the likes of what I saw tonight.

The night began like any other. I sat down in my tiny cottage on the cemetery grounds to go through my treasures from the day's burials. A small silver brooch and three small, gold rings. A tidy sum. I'm not proud of my actions, journal, but I will not compound my damnation by lying about them. Yes, I steal from the dead. The dead have no need of their possessions, after all, and I have seen nothing to prove to me that they will come looking for them again.

I was just preparing my evening meal when I heard the soft steps of someone in the yard. I thought it was another medical student or one of the professors looking for a body for their studies, so I grabbed my spade and lantern and went out into the cold.

At first, nothing appeared out of place. The gravestones and tombs made for a macabre scene, but to me this is home, and I feel at home among them. Still, something wasn't right. Perhaps it was the cold of the air or the feeling of being watched, but chills ran down my spine. I called out to the darkness. "Who's there?"

When no reply came, I ventured further into the cemetery. Sometimes body-snatchers come with pick and spade of their own and attempt to take the dead without paying for them, and I can't have that. I went around to the freshly entombed to check on them, but none of them were disturbed, their doors securely locked. I was walking back to my cottage when I saw the door to the Frankenstein tomb open, the chain split in two and lying on the cold soil.

I raised my lantern. "Hello!" I cried into the night, gripping my spade tightly.

In a groan that was as low and as lonely as the wind, a voice replied "Go away."

Thinking this a friend of the recently departed Frankensteins, I ventured closer to the tomb. Its peaked roof loomed above me and blocked out the light of the moon. I have been doing this job for more years than I can count, and journal, I can say with conviction that I have never before been afraid to enter a tomb before this night. I shined my lantern into the stagnant darkness, and my light fell upon the back of a man who was a great and imposing figure, made more so by his need to crouch to avoid the tall, slanted ceiling. I took a look at the man, and a look at my old spade, and pitched it aside.

The clatter of the falling spade made the man turn, and my light fell upon his hooded face. He had the remnants of great injury to his features, great stitches had once held him together, and I wondered if he had been in the recent troubles to the north. He looked as if he might hold a cannon against his mighty chest and fire it by sheer will alone. But then, looking closer, I saw the unmistakable countenance of misery. And as my light fell beyond him onto the stone slab, I saw the charred and rotting remains of a man, laid out with care, his arms forced into a repose of eternal rest.

"Sir," I said, finding my voice at last, "you cannot simply break into a tomb and leave a body behind, I'm afraid. This is the Frankenstein family's tomb."

The man looked me in the eye for the first time, and I saw the ghost of anger there, just for a moment, and then it was gone. "This is Victor Frankenstein," he replied, quietly. "He is all that was left of the family Frankenstein." He sighed, deeply, and looked back at the corpse.

"I see." I dug into my oiled greatcoat's pocket and brought forth every grave keeper's best friend: a small bottle of spirits, strong as the fires of hell. I uncorked the bottle and passed it, silently, to my companion. He looked down to the bottle, then over to me as if weighing my intentions. Then he took the bottle and drank a great quantity. He seemed to stop drinking as a thought struck him, and passed the bottle back to me. I took a sip and corked the now empty bottle, returning it to my greatcoat.

The man spoke. "The last time he and I stood here, he had sworn vengeance upon me. He had sworn to pursue me, sworn revenge for the life I had ravaged. He wished for me to drink deep of agony and of despair, and I think, finally, he has his wish, for without him I have no purpose. Without him, I have nothing for which to strive. I am as empty as his cold, lifeless heart."

Not knowing what to say, I cleared my throat and ventured "Was he a good man?"

He bent low and brushed the faded hair away from the corpse's face. "He was a great man of science, a great man of study and of books, but was he a good man?" He closed his eyes, and then shook his head. "No, he was not a good man. And yet I mourn him. As a son does a father, and as a mortal a fallen god, I mourn him, and that is enough." And then he knelt next to the body and placed a tender kiss upon its lips, and though it may have been the wind, I swear I heard him whisper "I'm sorry, father."

He then stood and turned to me, his cheeks moist but his face as solid and cold as the stone that surrounded us, and I admit I was again afraid. "Seal this place, grave keeper. Close me in, and never again open this tomb upon the light of day. I beg of you."

I could tell by the look in his eyes that he was in earnest, and yet something stirred within me. It was as if all the pity I could muster was suddenly reaching from my soul and resting upon this poor creature, who had, it seemed, seen his world collapse around him. I shook my head. "I cannot do as you ask," I said. Again the ghost of anger threatened to bloom upon the man's face, but I continued, driven by fear as much as by purpose. "You said you mourn this man as if he were your father, as if he were your god. And it seems to me that I don't know of any father nor god who would want such a fate for their son." I risked everything and reached a hand up to his shoulder and rested it there. "I'm sorry, my friend, I will not cause your doom."

The giant turned to look once again at the corpse, then glanced at my hand upon his shoulder. Finally, he looked down at me. "Friend?" he asked, as if tasting the word for the first time. He held my gaze as he seemed to debate something in his mind. Finally, he reached a decision. "Friend, then," he finished, and reached his great hand out to me.

I gripped him by the wrist as best I could, and he closed his hand around my entire forearm like an eclipse of flesh. He released his grip and gently moved me aside as if I were but a twig from a new branch in spring. As he reached the entrance of the tomb, he paused and spoke over his shoulder. "Thank you," he began, then seemed to hesitate. "…friend," he finished. He walked from the light of my lantern and into the cold, darkness of the night.

I returned to my cottage and fished my meal from the pot over the fire. I made myself a bowl, sat down, and began to work on these pages.

I fear my meal has grown cold with the telling.

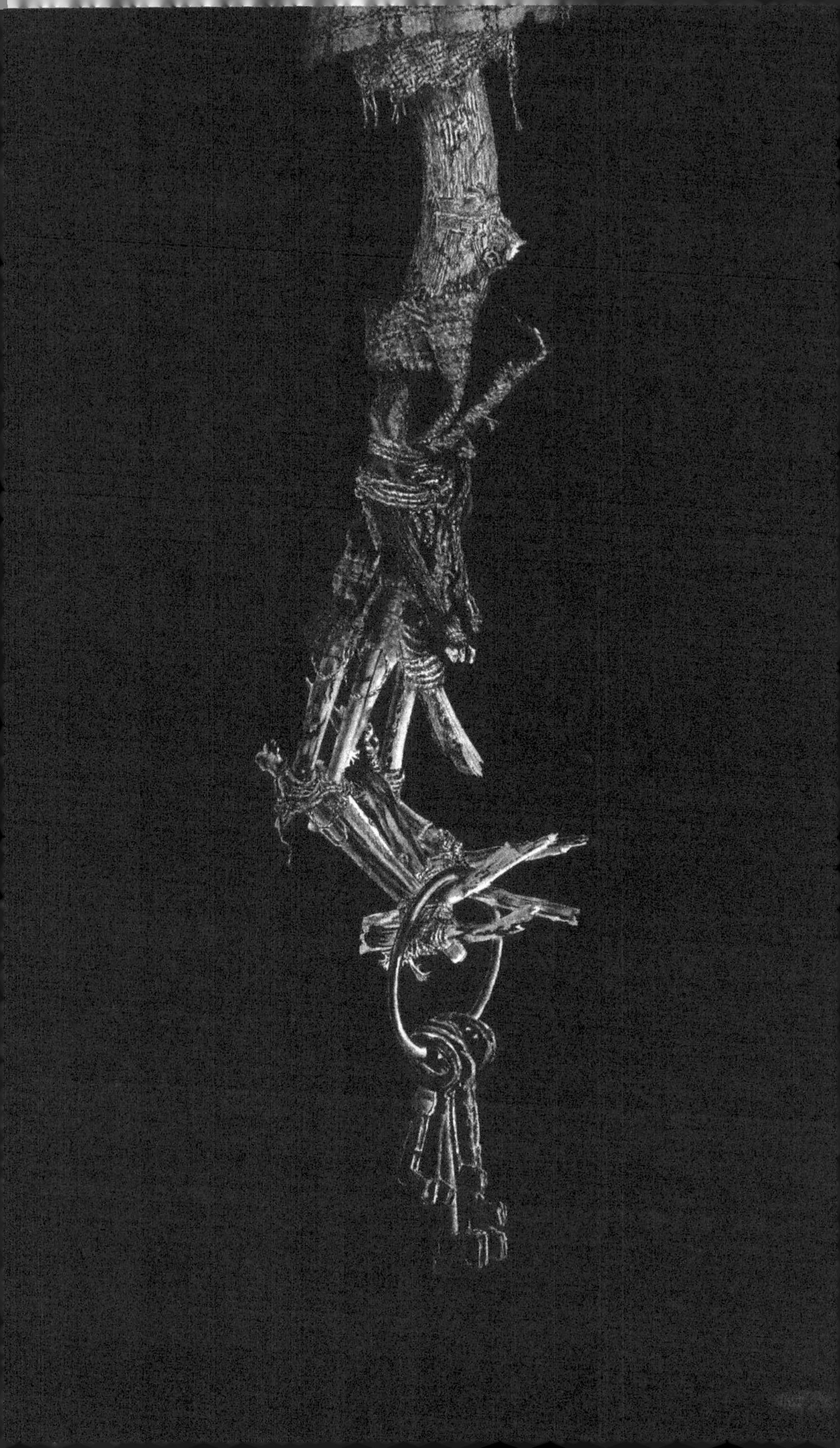

<u>Rust and Dust</u>

The property had been abandoned for centuries. Stories and legends were still being told about the old place: how there must have been a murder in the now crumbling manor house, or how the cellars were littered with bodies of a long-extinct family. One thing was for certain – nothing, not bird nor beast nor bug will dare cross the fence line and into the fields.

Hedra peered over an aged and crumbling wall, shielding her eyes from the autumn sun. The fields were a patchwork of gold and green, allowed to grow wild for the last few hundred years.

At least, that's what the property manager had told her when she bought the place. She spotted the manor house in the middle of the property, still undamaged by the ravages of time save for a partially collapsed roof. She wondered if any of the previous property managers had kept up on repairs.

She hopped onto the short wall and was just stepping off the other side and onto the property when the wind suddenly picked up and blew something into her eyes. She landed heavily on her side and elbow on the ground.

Cursing, she stood up. Her elbow throbbed and stung where the skin had torn. She turned and kicked the wall by way of revenge, then carried on toward the house.

The walls of the house were all large stone blocks. It didn't match any of the quarry stone she had seen in town. She wondered if the stone were taken from the fields themselves and used for building as the original owner had expanded the farm. There were windows all along the front of the house, filled with hand-poured glass. Shutters hung from several of them, though others had fallen off over time. *It's really not that bad,* she thought, taking it all in.

She walked to the front door and tried the latch, but it was locked. The manager had warned her about that, and had recommended bringing a locksmith on her first visit, but to Hedra, that seemed too easy. She wanted to explore, to adventure on her new lands, and what better way to begin than by breaking into her new house?

She walked around the building, picking her point of entry, wondering why none of the local kids had ever taken a rock to any of the windows. Finally, she found what she was looking for – a fairly easy climb along the large stones and windowsills up to the collapsed portion of the roof. She nodded to herself, and started climbing.

Her elbow protested the whole way up, and more than once forced her to find a better place to grip, but she made it to the top without harm and dropped into the space below.

She pulled a small flashlight from her pocket and shined it around the room. Rain had gotten into this area of the house for who knows how long, but the covered portions seemed to still be in surprising shape. She walked along the rafters to a small staircase leading down in the far corner.

She found herself in the kitchen. The air was musty and foul, the dust causing her to sneeze every now and then. *No bodies or bloodstains, so far,* she thought, walking through the kitchen and into a hallway. The hallway lead to some sort of parlor. The shelves were stripped bare. Whoever was last in here, either owner or thief, had taken everything from the room.

She walked over to a window and opened it. She pushed on the shutters to open them as well, but they came apart and clattered to the ground. She breathed deeply in the fresh, outdoor air, enjoying it all the more after being inside.

In the distance, in the middle of the field, a figure stood. "Hello!" Hedra called out, but the figure didn't respond or turn around to face her. She climbed out of the window and marched through the long grass out to meet them.

"Can I help you?" she asked as she approached, but the other person didn't stir. Hedra reached out and spun them around by the arm, then let out a short yelp.

"...A scarecrow," she said out loud to calm her nerves. "I'm talking to a scarecrow." She shook her head, but she had to admire the effort that went into its construction. It had clothing – a tweed shirt and jeans – legs, arms that hung at its sides. It even had fingers formed from old sticks and broken bones, lashed together with string.

Hanging from its fingers was a set of keys on a steel ring. Hedra laughed. *Someone obviously had a sense of humor,* she thought, picturing the original exchange as a drunken lark.

She took the keys and went back to the manor house, this time unlocking and opening the front door. It was time to get to work.

It was already late in the day. A month had gone by since she had last been to the manor house, and she couldn't be happier with the repairs that had been done. The roof was fixed, the shutters patched and replaced, power was ran to the house and lights installed, and the old wall that surrounded the property was repaired. She had movers bring her belongings and furniture from storage and into the house just last night, and tonight would be her very first stay at the house since she had bought it.

She still had no real plumbing to speak of, but the water pump to the well was built into the kitchen, so at least she had indoor water. She cooked herself a simple dinner, unpacked a few boxes, put away what she could, and then, tired from the journey here and from her own excitement, she went to bed.

She awoke and sat up in the darkness of her bedroom. There had been a sudden noise that woke her, she was sure of that, but now the house was eerily calm. She stood up and went to the window. The moonlight basked the field below in a pale gloom bright enough to see by, but too dark to make out many details.

Something was moving in the field. It appeared to be someone flailing around, spinning, dancing in a strange rhythm. Hedra put on a pair of pajamas against the evening's cold and went downstairs.

A crash rang out from the kitchen. "You clumsy oaf," a voice said in a self-depreciating tone, not even pretending to hide their presence. "His lordship will have my hide for sure."

Hedra opened the kitchen door from the stairs and turned on a light. There were several broken dishes lying on the floor, still rocking back and forth on jagged edges, but there was no-one else in the room. Hedra took a deep breath, then jumped the sound of a harpsichord filled the air. It seemed to be coming from the parlor. She grabbed a large kitchen knife and slowly made her way toward the tune.

She stood in the hallway and pressed her ear to the door to the parlor. She heard the murmur of a room-full of people, voices coming and going, gossip being spread, and through it all the harpsichord played. "More wine!" called a gruff, drunken voice somewhere in the room.

"Right away, sir," someone replied. Footsteps were crossing the room, headed toward Hedra. They stopped in front of the door. The latch moved, and the door slowly creaked open. Hedra peered into the room, empty except for her boxed-up possessions.

"How did you get into my house?"

Hedra turned around. There, standing at the foot of the main staircase, was a man in an old-fashioned military uniform. His hand rested on the hilt of his saber, which shined in the moonlight.

"I'm waiting," the man said.

"I... Your house?" Hedra said, stunned, gripping her kitchen knife tightly.

the man stomped his boot in a sudden tantrum. "I am lord Alfred, and you are in my house! I demand to know why you are here!"

Hedra thought for a moment. "Lord Alfred? But you're dead."

Lord Alfred walked toward her, his boots echoing on the wooden floor. When he was only a few paces away, he smiled. "Why would that make any difference?" he said, drawing and raising his saber.

Hedra ducked through the door into the parlor and locked it behind her. The room vibrated with the echo of laughter, and then the sound was gone. The sun shone through the window, illuminating a pleasant sitting room and the numerous books that lined the shelves.

A man in a black butler's uniform was busy dusting the shelves. He turned, saw Hedra, and deflated.

"Oh, no," he said. "You can't be here. If you're here, then Lord Alfred will have gone, and if he's gone, then-" The butler ran to the window and peered out into the field. Hedra fancied that she could see the color drain from his face. He turned to her. "You shouldn't have come."

Hedra stood in darkness once again, the books, the butler, and the chairs had all vanished, replaced by her own furniture and boxes. She stood still for several minutes, catching her breath. Then, she took a firm grip of the kitchen knife and went out of the parlor once again.

Lord Alfred was no longer around, and she let out a sigh of relief. She walked to the window and looked out on the field. The scarecrow was there, stuck to its pole, but whatever had been dancing in the field was gone. Hedra wondered if he ever existed at all.

The scarecrow turned its head to look directly at Hedra, standing in the window. Hedra gasped, and watched as the lifeless construct pulled itself free of the stake that held it in place, and slowly started to walk toward the house in jerking, flailing movements.

"You should have listened and left while you still could," a voice said from behind her. She turned and saw the butler standing there. He looked disappointed. "I really don't understand you people. We throw you off of walls, we collapse part of the building, we even lock the doors and throw away the key, but somehow, every so often, someone else comes along."

"What are you talking about?" Hedra asked.

"You. You come here, you break in, you rebuild, and for what? Is this the only ruin in the world these days? Are there no other houses available that you had to pick this one?"

"I don't understand. All I did was buy the property and move in."

The butler chuckled. "Nobody can buy this property. The owner is still here, and he's not inclined to sell."

"You mean Lord Alfred?" Hedra asked.

The butler smiled, sadly. "No. Lord Alfred didn't own this land anymore than you do. He's just... gone mad over time. He was raised as a baron, you see? He isn't used to not getting his way, and to lose out to that? To be kept here against his will? The embarrassment must have broken him."

"To lose to what?"

"To the owner." The butler moved to the window, watching the figure's halting approach. "The scarecrow."

"How can the scarecrow be the owner?"

The butler laughed. "There's no time," he said, then turned to Hedra once again. "If he catches you, you'll be stuck here with the rest of us." Under his breath, he added "At least I'll have someone else to talk to."

Hedra glared at the butler. "I have no intention of being stuck here with you forever," she said, looking at the scarecrow's progress. It was very close, now. "How do you stop it?"

Lord Alfred laughed from the top of the stairs. The butler rolled his eyes. "You don't stop it, idiot girl!" Lord Alfred shouted. "You get stopped *by* it. That scarecrow is older than this house. You may as well attempt to stop the wind!"

The scarecrow reached the door. It started pounding, shaking the wall.

Hedra ran upstairs to the bedroom just as the door burst inward. The scarecrow followed.

Hedra closed and locked the door with the house keys, then she pushed the bed against it. The top half of the door exploded in a hail of splinters. The scarecrow peered in at Hedra, its blank, lifeless expression piercing her soul like shards of ice.

She swiped at the scarecrow with the kitchen knife, but it didn't even try to avoid the strikes. She plunged the blade into its chest, and the scarecrow backhanded her further into the room.

Hedra landed heavily. When she got back to her feet, the scarecrow was already through the broken door. It corralled her toward the corner, never letting her dive to one side or the other. Hedra swung the house keys at it, using the heavy metal as a weapon.

When she could retreat no further, her back pressed into the corner, the scarecrow reached for her. In desperation, she threw the keys at it.

It was simple luck that the key ring looped around the scarecrow's outstretched hand.

The creature paused, holding perfectly still for several seconds before straightening out, turning around, and crawling back through the ruined door. Hedra followed at a distance.

The butler and Lord Alfred looked at the scarecrow as it passed them, the back to Hedra. "What did you do?" asked Lord Alfred.

Hedra shrugged and followed the scarecrow out the door.

She stepped out into daylight. The house behind her was gone. The stone property wall was new, the stones all freshly cut and mortared. A gate was just being installed. An important looking man strung a single key onto a steel ring and dangled it from the scarecrow's hand. "Guard it well," the man said, and turned away.

Then the house was built, and another man was adding a key to the ring that hung from the Scarecrows hand. The wall nearby had aged, but still stood strong and proud.

Then Lord Alfred appeared. The house was larger, now, but the wall had begun to fall to ruin, already. Lord Alfred added a third key to the ring, then he hung the ring from his own belt. The scarecrow's head turned to stare at Lord Alfred as he walked away...

Hedra stood in her pajamas in the cool moonlight of autumn, staring at an ancient scarecrow who watched the entry gate like a sentry. She thought she understood, now.

When she went back inside, Lord Alfred and the butler were gone, but she hadn't really expected them to wait for her. She was sure she would be seeing them around from time to time.

She went upstairs, cleared the wood fragments from her bed as best she could, and slept peacefully, knowing she had a powerful creature watching over her.

Acknowledgments

We would like to thank everyone who has helped us along the way while we put together this project. There was a lot of hair-pulling, a lot of sleepless nights, but in the end I think we produced something worthy of your time. We would both like to thank Oscar Diggs for allowing us to use and modify his font for our cover, and we would also like to thank Jay Charles for all of his help in cover design, flyers, posters... am I forgetting anything, Jay?

A special thank you from Sean to those who helped back our projects on Kickstarter, to Pink, who volunteered her time to edit my stories when she was having troubles of her own; to Grant and Jeff for coming to the rescue with recording equipment for the tour and audio book; to my coworkers at my day job, who pulled shifts when I was unable due to deadlines; to my father, who made sure I ate when I forgot what day it was; to my boss, who allowed me the time off to get not only the book finished, but to take it on tour out of the country; to everyone who answered a late-night question without asking me why; to everyone who encouraged me, however simply, along the way, you all have my deepest, and most heartfelt thanks.

And if you, reader, are still reading this after a tirade like that, I

would also like to thank you. Look at you. Reading the acknowledg-
ments page like the total badass you are. I like you.

209